Slocum returned [...] was too late. A fe[...] of dust—wrapped [...] doubt—move rapidly from the base of the hill and disappear into the distance.

He stood up and retrieved his hat. Two holes—an entry and an exit hole, both big enough to stick his little finger through—marred the crown.

All he'd wanted when he rode out here was to see Maddie again—and not incidentally get himself a real quality lay—but so far he'd buried a stranger, walked into a houseful of naked women about to geld some addlepated cowpoke, dickered with an angry mob of men, and now somebody was shooting at him.

And they'd ruined a perfectly good hat.

DON'T MISS THESE
ALL-ACTION WESTERN SERIES
FROM THE BERKLEY PUBLISHING GROUP

THE GUNSMITH *by J. R. Roberts*
Clint Adams was a legend among lawmen, outlaws, and ladies. They called him . . . the Gunsmith.

LONGARM *by Tabor Evans*
The popular long-running series about U.S. Deputy Marshal Long—his life, his loves, his fight for justice.

SLOCUM *by Jake Logan*
Today's longest-running action Western. John Slocum rides a deadly trail of hot blood and cold steel.

BUSHWHACKERS *by B. J. Lanagan*
An action-packed series by the creators of Longarm! The rousing adventures of the most brutal gang of cutthroats ever assembled—Quantrill's Raiders.

JAKE LOGAN

SLOCUM AND THREE WIVES

JOVE BOOKS, NEW YORK

SLOCUM AND THREE WIVES

A Jove Book / published by arrangement with
the author

PRINTING HISTORY
Jove edition / August 1999

All rights reserved.
Copyright © 1999 by Penguin Putnam Inc.
This book may not be reproduced in whole or in part,
by mimeograph or any other means, without permission.
For information address: The Berkley Publishing Group,
a division of Penguin Putnam Inc.,
375 Hudson Street, New York, New York 10014.

The Penguin Putnam Inc. World Wide Web site address is
http://www.penguinputnam.com

ISBN: 0-515-12569-5

A JOVE BOOK®
Jove Books are published by The Berkley Publishing Group,
a division of Penguin Putnam Inc.,
375 Hudson Street, New York, New York 10014.
JOVE and the "J" design
are trademarks belonging to Penguin Putnam Inc.

PRINTED IN THE UNITED STATES OF AMERICA

10 9 8 7 6 5 4 3 2 1

1

Slocum worked the final rock down into place, then stepped back from the mounded grave. It was never a pleasant thing to find a body, particularly when you were in the middle of the Arizona desert, and particularly when that body had been dead for at least a week, and the coyotes had been feasting and the buzzards had been picking.

He'd found what pieces were left and gathered them up—at least, those that hadn't been dragged too far to find—and scraped a shallow trough in the hard desert soil. He'd finished with a cairn of rocks.

He folded his collapsible shovel, stuck it back behind his saddle, under his bedroll, and took down his canteen.

Thirsty work, grave-digging. At least the worst of the summer had gone by, he told himself. Best to be grateful for small blessings.

Also, it was a good thing he wasn't more than fifteen or sixteen miles from Three Wives, because he was down to his last half canteen of water. He took a long swig, swishing the liquid back and forth through his teeth before he swallowed, then carefully poured water into the cup of his hand and offered it to his horse.

It was a five-year-old Appaloosa mare, and a fine one: nearly fifteen hands tall with bottom to spare, and a kind, intelligent look in her eyes. Her coat was a glossy jet-black, and over her hips was a white blanket, splashed with black spots as big as the stamp of a man's fist. Too nice a horse to be looking as trail-weary as she did at this moment.

He poured out the rest of the canteen and offered it to the mare, who drank gratefully.

''That's the last of it, Bess,'' he said, and slung the empty canteen's strap over his saddlehorn. It banged against the leather skirts of the saddle.

The dead man's horse had been nowhere to be found, but Slocum had discovered a piece of paper in his otherwise empty—and coyote-chewed—wallet. A card really, a card smelling faintly of verbena. The kind that high-toned women back East left on silver salvers when they came to call.

On the back of it, someone had written in pencil, ''Three Wives, A.T. Please come with all haste.''

And the name engraved on the front had really thrown him for a loop, because it was the name of the woman he was riding to Three Wives to see: Maddie O'Hara.

He'd met her a couple of years back—found her on the desert actually, staggering and sunburnt and half dead from dehydration. She'd led him into a pack of trouble, all right, but he had to admit that she was worth it.

Worth her weight in bobcats too, once you got her riled.

She was more full-to-the-brim with lies than a Kansas City cardsharp, and six times as good-looking with those blue eyes and jet-black hair. And that face. Shaped like a heart, it was. She had the body to go with it too, and knew all the tricks to keep a man happy—she'd come down from Chicago, from a high-class brothel.

He gathered she'd enjoyed her work there.

Well, he wanted more than to see her, even though the little raven-haired Irish vixen was definitely a sight to behold. A lot more than looking, that's what he was after. A couple of days with him and Maddie in a locked room and no furniture but a bed would be fine, for starters.

Hell, they didn't even need the bed.

He found he was smiling, and nipped it in the bud. Hardly the place or the time for it, considering the tattered thing he'd just buried.

"Come with all haste?" he muttered as he stepped up on his mare. "What have you gotten yourself into this time, Maddie?"

Tipping his hat to the stone-piled grave a last time, he said, "*Vaya con Dios,* pardner. Hope you were all the way dead when the coyotes started gnawing on you."

He eased the mare into a jog, and rode off through the shimmering heat toward Three Wives.

Maddie O'Hara quickly wiped her sodden brow on her sleeve, then handed the spent rifle to the equally perspiration-drenched woman hunched a few feet away, behind the shield of an upturned table. Her furniture was never going to be the same.

"Hurry up, Charity!" she cried. Another slug tore through the wood of the shuttered window above her and shattered a glass kitten on the mantel.

"I'm going as fast as I can!" wailed Charity, a buxom young redhead whose face was streaked with tears. "There's only one of me loading, and two of you shooting!"

She shoved a loaded Winchester into Maddie's hands. "I never should've come here! I never should have let you talk me into it! I never should have left Chicago! I never—"

"Shut up and load something!" called the third and final occupant of the house—a full-figured honey blonde—over the whine and dull *splat* of bullets. From the far window, also shuttered, she said, "At least you're safe, Charity. At least you're behind that tabletop! Good God! If I'd'a known Mace was gonna take on this way, I just would've let him sing the damn song instead of filling him full of bird shot!"

"That's enough, Jane," Maddie shouted sternly. "Charity, get cracking or we won't have any more need of loaded weapons." The comment wasn't lost on Charity, who absorbed herself in cramming cartridges into the rifle's chamber.

Whatever possessed those idiots out there to start shooting? Maddie thought. *And what in heaven's name ever convinced me that this would work?*

Grim-lipped, she rose, stuck the Winchester's barrel through a gun-port in the shutter, sighted down on the water trough, and squeezed the trigger. Water streamed from the newly made hole— the water trough was beginning to look like a sieve—and she cursed under her breath.

I was out of my mind to bring Charity and Jane and Ann-Elizabeth out here. Movement in a cluster of palo verde ten feet from the trough caught her eye, and she fired at it. The shot was returned, and she ducked just in time to avoid a cheek full of splinters.

Jane said, "Got it," and fired three rounds, then quickly ducked as a barrage of lead opened a hole in her shutter as big as a man's head and let a wide beam of dusty light into the house.

"Jeez Louise!" Jane shouted, staring upward at the sunlight pouring through the new rift. "Don't these lunatics have any sense of chivalry? Where were their mothers, for God's sake? Shooting at a house full of helpless females—"

"Hey, you got one!" whooped Maddie. Then, suddenly disgusted, she said, "Aw, rats. He's only wounded."

"Shoot him again, Maddie," said Charity's small voice. A glance to the side showed damp red hair clinging to the delicate hands that covered her eyes. "Shoot them all! Make them go away!"

"My, my," said a new and wholly unexpected—and unwelcome—voice. "Ain't this a pretty picture?"

Maddie wheeled toward it, bringing the rifle with her, but it was too late. Mace Cantrell already had Jane by the throat. He held her body against him like a shield, and his pistol's barrel was pressed to her temple. He was grinning like it was Christmas, the stupid bastard.

Sighing, Maddie set the Winchester down.

"That's better, honey," Mace said with a smirk. She wanted to slap it off his face, but she stood her ground. There was Jane to consider, not to mention Charity, who was cowering on the floor, her limbs trembling.

"Ought to keep a better guard on them back windows," he went on. "Took out them Meskins'a yours in nothing flat."

Oh, no! she thought. *Poor Pedro and Geraldo.* But she didn't let it show on her face. There'd be time enough to see to the damage later on. Right now, she had to think of the living. Mace had gone flat-out crazy!

She said, "Nothing flat, Mace? Took you nearly twenty minutes."

He sniffed. " 'Bout as long as it's gonna take you to pack up and move to that place Mr. Loomis's got for you in town. You gals can open up shop tomorrow. Course," he added with a leer, "I'm comin' along with y'all. I got me a hanker to be Miss Jane's first customer, in case y'all hadn't noticed. In fact, I've been wonderin' what it'd be like to take you all on at the same time."

Isn't that just like a man, Maddie thought. *Eyes ten times bigger than his . . .* Suddenly, she smiled at him. He was talking a whole lot bigger than he ever had before—and ever would again, if she had anything to do with it. How dare he come strutting in here like the cock of the walk!

Still smiling slyly, she pushed the damp hair out of her eyes. "Why wait till we get to town, Mace? I've kinda got an urge myself. Gunfire brings out the wild side of me." She began to unbutton her bodice. "C'mon, ladies," she said to the others. "Let's show Mace what he won."

Indecision flickered over Mace's face, but by then Maddie had already unbuttoned and opened the front of her dress.

Mace swallowed hard, his Adam's apple bobbing.

"Maddie?" said Charity's voice, quavering with doubt.

"Just do it," hissed Jane. She was still in

Mace's grip, but she seemed, at least, willing to play along.

Maddie wondered if Jane was wishing she could trade this for a little of Mace's out-of-tune warbling. To Maddie's mind, a little lost sleep was sure better than a gun to your head.

Charity began to fumble with her buttons.

"You'd better tell your friends to hold their fire for a bit, Mace," said Maddie, stepping out of her dress. She opened the top of her camisole and let it drop to her waist, exposing her breasts.

Mace swallowed again. "I'm in!" he yelled, after some trouble with his throat. "You boys just hang on a couple'a minutes! Everything's jim-dandy!" Then he turned his attention to Charity, who was trying to get out of her dress without getting to her feet. "You, Miss Charity. You stand up and kick all them rifles over to the corner, hear?"

From outside, one of the men shouted, "Mace? Mace, you all right?"

"Righter'n rain!" he called back. "You boys give me 'bout ten minutes, and then I got a treat for you!" He pushed Jane from him, and at the same time let loose with a Rebel yell that shook the paintings on the walls. "C'mon, ladies, let's see some skin!"

"But Mike's bleedin'!" came the voice from outside.

"Not much!" replied Mace, his eyes on Jane.

"He'll live!" He still held the pistol in one hand, but with the other he freed his gunbelt, then went to work on his pants. "Now, shut up out there and let a man tend to business!"

"To the spoils of war," cooed Maddie coyly, and dropped her bloomers.

"Goddamn, girl," Mace breathed, his watery gaze moving to Maddie and traveling up, then down, then up her body again. "I ain't never see'd an all-over naked female before." He swallowed, hard. "You're a regular feast, Miss Maddie."

From behind her, Jane said, "What about me?"

Maddie could tell, by Mace's dropped jaw, that she had lost a good bit of her clothing as well.

"Am I a feast too, Mace darlin'?" Jane purred.

Maddie saw Mace's fingers eased their grip on his pistol, but he didn't drop it. *How annoying,* she thought, and lowered her head slightly to look up at him through her lashes. She kept on smiling. "Might's well get started, darlin'," she breathed, and took a step toward him.

Mace's pants sank to the floor, although he remained standing. He looked confused—actually, it was his natural state—which was just the way Maddie wanted him.

"If you're wondering where to point that pistol, baby," Maddie cooed, placing her hands on his filthy vest, "point it at lil ol' Charity there." She leaned on tiptoes to his ear and whispered, "She craves the danger."

Behind her, she heard Charity's whine of complaint.

She ignored it, and slid down Mace's body, felt him shiver when her bare breasts ruffled the hair on his legs, heard him gasp when he felt her breath on his cock.

"Not yet, baby," she murmured, and slid lower still. Above, Jane had moved in and was distracting him, peppering kisses over his face, pulling at his shirt. Good old Jane. Always quick on the uptake, that one.

Maddie slithered all the way to the floor and began nuzzling Mace's knees and inner thighs, but her hand was lower, finding the puddle of his britches, searching along the belt.

At last her fingers found the leather sheath. She slipped the knife free, and just as quickly brought the point up to bear against his testicles.

"Ow!" Mace yelped, and pushed Jane away. "Don't you whores go usin' your teeth or I'll—" He blinked with almost comical slowness when he saw the blade threatening his family jewels. His erection withering, he whispered, "Aw, shit."

Maddie gave him a little poke with the tip of the knife. "Shame on you, Mace. Trying to take advantage of three helpless little girls from out of town." She clucked her tongue.

Jane, who had already relieved Mace of his pistol, said, "Rope?"

"I think so," replied Maddie.

"Can I *please* put my clothes back on?" whimpered Charity. "I mean, he's not even interested in me, is he? It's all Jane, Jane, Jane."

Maddie rolled her eyes. "Oh, for the love of—"

"Hold it!" Jane shouted, in a voice far more imperious than any naked woman should use—even if, Maddie thought, that naked woman is holding a gun.

She peeked through the inverted V of Mace's quivering legs, and looked back into the shadowy hallway. Another one had come in the back. Well, this time they had the drop on him.

"Tell your friend to come out of there," she said to Mace, and pressed the knifepoint more firmly against its target. "Tell him to come out easy, with empty hands."

His face blanched, his privates shriveled, Mace began, "C-come out e-easy—"

"Maddie?" the new man said, interrupting him. He stepped forward into the light, surveyed the room, and immediately pushed back his hat. "Criminy, Maddie. First I find two stove-up Mexicans by the back stoop, and next I come in here and find everybody stark naked. I'm beginning to think maybe it's not such a good idea to come callin' unannounced!"

"Oh, you beautiful rat!" she cried. Dropping the knife, she scrambled between Mace's legs and threw herself up and into Slocum's arms.

2

After hearing the gunfire and spying on the battle from a rock a quarter mile distant, Slocum had ridden, then walked, then crawled his way from brush clump to scrub tree to cactus patch, and finally to the sprawling ranch house's back door. He'd realized Maddie was in trouble when he found the note on the body in the desert, but he hadn't realized that danger was so imminent.

He'd come into the house prepared for anything. Well, he thought he had. But now he had Maddie, stark naked and slithering around in his arms like a greased and happy eel, and there were two other women, equally naked, staring at him with open mouths. There was a desperado without pants quivering in the center of the ruined parlor, and outside, a bunch of rowdies sat around smoking and laughing, as if they were waiting their turn at a one-tub town's bathhouse. Well, maybe more like they were waiting for the only whore in two hundred miles.

Reluctant though he was to do it, he pried Maddie's lips away from his and said, "Darlin', what in the name of thunder is going on?"

Dryly, the blond said, "A little problem with our friend here." She was a blond all the way to her toes, Slocum noticed admiringly. Round-hipped and full-breasted, she held a Colt Peacemaker on Mr. No Pants as if standing around in her birthday suit was something she'd gotten used to—and bored with—years ago.

"Jane," his dark-haired Maddie said, giving his waist a little squeeze, "meet Slocum. Slocum, meet Jane."

He touched the brim of his hat with a finger while he watched a bead of sweat run down between Jane's breasts to her belly. "Pleased, ma'am." He didn't remember ever having meant it more.

Across the room, a little redhead struggled into her drawers, although not fast enough to keep him from seeing that she'd never had the need of a henna rinse. Strawberry everywhere.

"And this other young lady?" he asked.

"That's Charity," Maddie said.

Charity didn't look up. She tied her drawers and began sifting through a pile of petticoats, although she was still nude from the waist up. "Die," she mumbled, her attention on the petticoats, "I could just die."

"How do, Miss Charity," Slocum said.

"Oh, botheration," Charity remarked, although he was fairly certain the comment was aimed at the petticoats rather than at him.

"Slocum," Maddie said, "leave it to you to show up at the exact right moment."

"Could you talk and tie him up at the same time?" Jane asked, motioning with the Colt at Mr. No Pants.

With a sigh, Maddie moved away from him and pulled a sash from one of the curtains that was still hanging. As she began binding Mr. No Pants's wrists, she said, "This is Mace. Works over on the Loomis place. Mace is usually an easy fellow to get along with—well, except when he's serenading Jane at three in the morning—but today he got a little ornery. Say hello, Mace."

Mace grunted weakly, and whispered, "Could I just pull my britches up?"

"Sorry, Mace," said Maddie, all business. "No time to cover your butt, let alone anything else. Besides, I kind of like the way those trousers hobble you." She gave the sash a final tug, then pushed him back until he sat down, hard, in a caned back chair.

Probably had a cane seat too, Slocum thought. That was going to smart.

"Like I said, Mace here works for Carl Loomis," she continued as she bent and picked up her clothes from the floor. "And Carl Loomis is the biggest skunk-sucking sonofabitch in the county."

"You whores shouldn't be sayin' bad things about Mr. Loomis," said Mace, who was apparently feeling a bit better now that he realized he wasn't going to be gelded. His eyes were glued to Maddie's backside.

"Let me kill him, Maddie," said Jane, glaring.

"Now, Jane," Maddie scolded, "you know you've already shot your quota for the week."

Jane snorted.

At the sight of Mace's face, Slocum covered his mouth. It wasn't the best time to laugh, considering there were still four or five men outside who were going to be getting real antsy anytime now.

"Maddie?" he urged.

"After you and I finished that business down south and I came back up here, everything was just peachy for a while," she went on, dressing as she talked. He felt a little sadder with every stitch that went back on. "For a couple of years, in fact. Of course, Daddy had leached out most of the gold for that crackpot idea of his, but there was enough that I never went hungry, and that I could send for Jane and Charity here. Well, and Ann-Elizabeth too."

Slocum said, "Send for them? And who's Ann-Elizabeth?" If there was another naked woman lurking in the shadows, he wanted to see her.

He noticed that Jane had set aside the gun, but hadn't made the first move toward finding her clothes. She'd cleared the rubble from a settee and sat there spraddle-legged, idly stroking a breast with one hand while she stared at Mace, who had turned beet red. And who, suffice it to say, was once again fully aroused.

Slocum cleared his throat and made himself look away, reminding himself that it was Maddie he was here to see. And he'd had already seen more of her—and faster—than he'd hoped.

Maddie wriggled into her dress. Ignoring his question about the other girl, she said, "They worked at the place I used to work at. At Felicity's place in Chicago. Guess I don't have to explain why they wanted to leave."

He shook his head. "No." All Jane's attention was focused on poor Mace, who stared at her as she stroked herself, her hand between her open legs. If her goal was to get Mace to embarrass himself, it looked as if she was about to succeed.

"Oh, for God's sake, Jane," Maddie said suddenly. "Put something on and quit teasing that poor helpless boy."

"He wasn't so helpless when he came in here waving that gun around," Jane said, without taking her eyes from Mace.

"And you, Charity," Maddie said. "Get busy—"

"Hello the house!" came the call from outside. "Hey, Mace! Everything all right in there?"

"Answer him," said Slocum, glad for something to do besides trying to avert his eyes. Not that he minded nudity, or even that the girls minded him looking, but it was surely a distraction and a half from the crisis at hand.

Mace made a tiny whimpering sound. "Please!" he whined, eyes still pinned to Jane, who reluctantly picked up her camisole and began to pull it on. "I'm gonna have me a case of the blue balls!"

"Better than no balls at all," Slocum said. He drew his gun and pointed it square at Mace's chest. "Answer them. Tell them five minutes."

"Five minutes!" Mace obediently barked. "Five more minutes, an' then they're all yours, boys!"

"What?"

Maddie was at his side. "Never mind, Slocum. It's just something we said—and he said—before. I'll explain it all—and you can explain how you happened to turn up at just the right moment—but first, we've got a little problem to take care of."

Naked women, dead men in the desert, and more naked women. It was a pattern he wasn't any too keen on—although he could have lived with just the naked-women part. After he got this little "problem" cleaned up, he was going to have a few choice words with Maddie. Maybe give her a good spanking. Maybe something else.

But first, he had to get around the backside of this mob.

He'd circled the house by going round the far

side of the barn, and by now he guessed that his five minutes were about up. Any minute the men would be trooping off across the front yard and up to the stoop, expecting a high old time in that shot-up parlor of Maddie's.

He wished Maddie'd had time to explain everything—even part of it—before he willingly stuck his dick in the proverbial wringer, but there you were. Now all he had to do was to disarm five men who were, to put it mildly, going to resist the procedure.

He was within fifteen feet of them, crouched behind a patch of prickly pear. Their backs were to him, and he could hear snatches of their conversation, most of which concerned which girl was going to do what to whom, and who was going to do what to which girl. Unnoticed by the men, he held up his arm and waved once at the house.

At the signal, Maddie opened the front door. At least, he saw with relief, she'd put all her clothes back on. He was going to have to talk to her about that later, preferably when they were alone together and she had them off again.

When Maddie opened the door, the men rose as one. Two took off their hats. Slocum could practically hear them licking their lips from behind the prickly pear. Grinning, he shook his head, and stood up.

"Not today, boys," he announced.

As a body, they spun toward him, but he already

had his Colt in one hand and one of Maddie's Winchesters dangling in the other, and nobody was fool enough to draw on him.

"Shit!" muttered one of the men, a big hombre with five days of dark chin stubble.

Slocum smiled. "That about says it, I reckon. Now, drop the gunbelts, if you wouldn't mind," he drawled. "Well, you'd best drop 'em anyway. Got your backside covered too, in case you got any ideas otherwise."

Up on the porch, Maddie cranked a round into the chamber of the rifle that Charity had just handed to her.

That sound was what got them moving. Gunbelts fell into the low brush, raising the fine, powdery dust with dull thuds and thumps.

"Mr. Loomis ain't gonna like this," said Chin Stubble.

"People like Loomis rarely do," Slocum replied dryly, although he had not the slightest idea who Loomis was—other than that these boys worked for him—or what any of this was about. "Now, back off a few feet from those guns, boys." He looked past them, to the house. "Maddie? You can bring Mace out now."

"Them whores better not have killed Mace!" cried an adolescent, breaking voice. It came from the youngest of Loomis's men, a pimply-faced blond kid whose left upper arm was bleeding.

"Nobody's dead," Slocum said, disgust creeping into his tone, "no thanks to you fellas. Ain't you ashamed to be sending bullets into a house full of women? And what was it? Six against three?"

"Five," Chin Stubble piped up. "Five with them Mex hands they got working for 'em."

Just then, Mace stumbled out onto the porch, nudged by the business end of Jane's rifle. Jane looked as if she'd be more than delighted to kill him where he stood, and Mace was bright red and fumbling with his britches.

"Out!" shouted Jane. "Out, you tone-deaf bastard!" She poked him with the barrel.

Mace fell off the porch and landed on his side with a billow of dust, but managed to keep one hand on his sagging pants as he scrambled to his feet.

Slocum made a mental note to ask Maddie about this singing business, and also about Jane. Seemed like she couldn't make up her mind about men, and was bent on either seduction or murder. However, he focused his attention on the group in front of him and said, "How far is it back to where they came from, you reckon?"

Chin Stubble gave him a growly look, but the blond kid said, "Three mile, give or take. Mace, you get any?"

"Shut up, Mike," Mace grumbled. He'd fastened his pants and belt and joined the group by this time.

"Maddie?" Slocum called over them. "Go round the barn and smack their horses on the rumps. Send 'em toward home."

As Maddie trotted off toward the barn, Mace said, "You can't—"

"Just did," Slocum said. "To tell you the truth, boys, I don't know the particulars of what's goin' on out here. But I can tell right off that you boys are in the wrong. First off, you're shooting at a bunch of women."

"Whores!" cried the blond kid called Mike, his voice trying to go to two octaves at once. "They're just a pile'a whores!"

"We work for Mr. Carl Loomis himself and—" Chin Stubble began angrily.

"Shut up," Slocum growled, cutting him off. "I figured both' a those things out. But it ain't no excuse for ungentlemanly behavior." In the distance, he heard Maddie shouting, and then the sound of galloping hooves. He twitched the Colt in the direction of the blond kid. "How's that arm?"

"S' okay," the kid answered, and Slocum thought he was telling the truth. The bullet must have just grazed him, for only a small amount of blood showed on his sleeve.

"All right then, gents," Slocum said, motioning all of them out of the brush and down the gentle slope, away from the house. "Start walking."

Chin Stubble scowled, and it was the kind of

scowl that says paragraphs. "What's your name, mister?"

"Slocum," he replied evenly. "John Slocum. Yours?"

"Ed Barlow," Chin Stubble growled menacingly. "Remember it."

Slocum could see that the situation was spiraling down into cheap melodramatics, and he just shook his head. "Don't tell me," he said wearily. "You're going to kill me, right?"

Barlow squinted at him. "That's pretty much the size of it, Slocum."

Slocum sighed. "Get moving. All of you."

3

Slocum lifted both hands over his head and shouted, "One at a time!"

The women and the Mexican hands all shut up at once, granting Slocum a moment of peace. It was, however, short-lived, because five seconds later they all began again.

He shoved back his chair, stood up, and yelled, "I'm going outside, damn it. I'm going outside, and I'm gonna throw that saddle back on my horse and ride the hell out of here just as fast as I can, if y'all can't talk one person at a goddamn time!"

They all shut up again, and this time Charity snorted through her nostrils and went back to trying to fix the curtains. Jane made a face at him, but went to help Charity. The Mexican hands looked at each other, then slumped resignedly back in their bandages.

That left him with Maddie, who stood facing him, her arms crossed and her toe tapping. "You don't have to be rude, Slocum," she said.

He breathed a sigh. "Neither do you." He reached over and with a heave, pulled the table right side up again. Then he sat down and ran his hand over its bullet-splintered top. He gestured to another fallen chair, which Maddie righted, then plopped down in.

"All right," he said. "Talk to me."

Charity and Jane both dropped the curtains and started babbling, and he closed his eyes and shouted, "Just Maddie, damn it!"

One of the hands stifled a laugh.

Slocum flicked his eyes to the corner, where both Pedro and Geraldo sat on the settee—Pedro with a bandaged arm and bandaged leg, and Geraldo with a bandaged head. Each looked at the other, then at Slocum, then shrugged as if to say that *they* certainly hadn't said anything. They were halfway into a bottle of mescal—to kill the pain, Maddie said when she gave it to them—and it had turned them into a couple of comedians.

"We'll talk later," Slocum said to them, then turned his attention to Maddie. She was just as beautiful as he remembered: sky-colored eyes, fine features, that rosy, bow-shaped mouth, the widow's peak that gave her face a heart shape. And that initial glimpse he'd had of her led him to believe the rest of her was just as fine as he remembered too.

"You, darlin'," he said, and his voice mellowed, tempered by thoughts of his hands cupping her rose-tipped breasts, her long, lean legs wrapping around his hips. "Talk to me. What the hell's going on?"

"I brought Charity and Jane and Ann-Elizabeth out from Chicago," she began without preamble. "We were going to try to make a go of it, to go straight. Pedro and Geraldo did the blasting and the heaviest work, and we all worked the shafts. We did fine, didn't we?" she asked, turning toward Pedro and Geraldo.

Geraldo nodded. "Extra fine. Pedro bought himself a fine new roan horse, and every month I send money to my sister in Chihuahua." He shrugged. "Anyway, I used to."

Slocum sent him a dirty look, and he shut up again.

Maddie's fine brows were knitted as she stared at the tabletop and her folded hands, and Slocum waited. At last, she said, "Then there wasn't any more gold. Just like that. I guess we cleaned it all out. Or Daddy did, before us." She looked up at him. "We were just about to get started in sheep, when—"

"Sheep?" Slocum broke in.

"Yes, sheep," she said testily. "Don't tell me you're one of those anti-sheep idiots too!"

He held up his hands. "Not me," he said, thinking about his chances of getting laid tonight. He could be crazy about sheep if it brought Maddie O'Hara to his bed. "You just surprised me," he added. "And I didn't see any sheep when I rode up."

"That's because they're not here yet," she said,

propping her head on one hand. "And they're not here yet because of Carl Loomis."

"You mentioned that name before."

Across the room, Jane spat out a few choice cuss words, ending with, "The vile bastard."

"Exactly," said Maddie.

"The boys who shot up your house mentioned him too," Slocum said. "What's Carl Loomis got to do with your sheep?"

"He wants Three Wives to have a whorehouse," she replied, as if that explained everything.

Slocum sighed and rubbed at the bridge of his nose. "I think you're leaving a whole lot out, Maddie. Like the entire middle. For instance, where's this Ann-Elizabeth? And how'd we get from no sheep to a whorehouse?"

"Ann-Elizabeth!" Maddie snorted dismissively. "The traitor! She doesn't have anything to do with this, though. It's Carl Loomis. He not only runs this town, he's head of the County Cattlemen's Association," she said, as if talking to a slow child. "They don't like sheep."

Slocum gritted his teeth. "And?"

"And Three Wives gets snowed in every winter," said Charity.

"The only women in town," interjected Geraldo, who by this time was slurring his words, "are Señora Hubbard, who is seventy-two, and Señora Carmody, who is sixty-three—"

"She has nice legs for the old lady, Geraldo," Pedro broke in. "Dixon Blake, at the livery? He told me he saw her ankle one time." He took another slug of mescal.

"And Señora French, who is Felix French's wife," Geraldo said, and punctuated it with a hiccup. "A man who is wise would not wish to mess with Felix French, even if his woman was not ugly and also bald as a hen's egg, which Señora French is." He took the bottle back from Pedro and hugged it to his chest. "It is very sad," he mumbled.

Slocum rolled his eyes. "If there are only three women in town besides you, why the hell doesn't somebody—"

"No one will come here, that's why," Maddie said, as if she'd read his mind. She was angrily drumming her fingers on the tabletop. "Women are scarce out here in the Territory anyhow—even scarcer in Three Wives—and the men are so butt-ugly, uneducated, and plain rude that none of them can get a woman without paying for it."

She stopped drumming her fingers, and put both hands flat on the table. "Just look at what you rode into today, Slocum. Where else would the menfolk get so low-down that they'd think the only way to get a woman to spread her legs is to shoot her first so she can't run away?"

Slocum still wasn't convinced, but he decided to leave it for later. He said, "And the sheep?"

"It's an excuse," Charity piped up in her fluty little voice. She'd been sweeping up the splinters from the floor, and she paused to lean on her broom. "It's just an excuse to beat us so far down that we'll take him up on his offer. Mr. Loomis, that is."

Slocum turned in his chair. Charity was probably only twenty and looked even younger. With her bee-stung lips, coffee-and-cream eyes, and riotous cloud of red hair, she looked as if she'd just stepped out of a painting by Titian.

Slocum asked, "What's his offer?"

"The house in town," Jane said before Charity could answer. He noticed for the first time that Jane was the tallest of the women by a good four inches. He'd noticed the high cheekbones and intense blue eyes before, but not the height. Of course, he figured that he had the excuse of being somewhat distracted by her other charms.

And he still hadn't begun to figure out just what her game was.

"You should see it," Jane went on, her voice filled with disdain. "This fancied-up, curlicued house, big as you please and smack dab on the town square, with a big sign out front that says, 'Three Wives Gaming Parlor—Opening Soon!' "

"Just as soon as he can get us in there," muttered Charity.

Jane continued. "He's got it all fancified with gingerbread and doodads and gingham curtains.

Feather beds and mirrors, I hear. Painted it bright pink on the outside.''

She snorted in disgust. ''Working whores, available twenty-four hours a day, for every syphilitic, pimple-faced, bowlegged, bad-breathed, unwashed-for-months hand that he's got on his place, that's what Loomis wants.''

Charity shook her head. ''Now, Jane,'' she said in her small, breathy voice. ''You don't know for a fact that they've all got Cupid's Itch.''

Jane waved a broom at her, and Charity went back to work.

''He has no intention of marrying off his men, Slocum,'' Maddie added, sitting back and ignoring the both of them. ''He wants to keep this place wide open, for his cattle as well as his hands. He figures that if he can offer us to keep them satisfied, those boys are going to be a whole lot happier to come down from the line camps.''

''After all,'' Charity offered again, with a tilt of her head, ''we *were* the prettiest women in Chicago. And I'll bet we're the prettiest women east of the Mississippi.''

''Brother,'' Jane muttered.

Maddie rolled her eyes. ''Well, I don't know about that, Charity, but we're a sight better than the back end of a longhorn range cow.''

A lot less bony too, Slocum thought, *though I'd be hard pressed to bet on which of the two could do more damage if you snuck up behind her in the dark.* He smiled, despite himself. *You'd think these boys would be fair delighted to see some nice, tame sheep. . . .*

Jane wasn't paying attention to his smile, though. She said, "He wants us to fail, the son-ofabitch. He wants us to come crawling to that cracker-box bordello of his." She was working herself up into a right state, Slocum's daddy would have said. Rage fairly oozed from her.

"As if I'd lower myself! Hell, I've screwed heads of state! Even a prince one time, for God's sake! I'm not about to come out of retirement to start doing a bunch of filthy cowhands for two bits a pop—or worse, for free!"

"Calm down, Jane," Maddie soothed. "Nobody's going to make you—"

"They'd better not," said Jane, and Slocum could tell she had control of herself again. "They'd just better not."

"Anyway," Maddie said, turning toward him, "that's why every time we try to bring sheep in, they end up sold to someplace else or dead on the desert or sent to market."

"What I can't figure out," Slocum said, "is why the hell you just don't—"

"I even hired a man," Maddie said, ignoring him. "A gunfighter named Taylor, Grant Taylor. Ever heard of him?"

Slocum shook his head.

"Well, I'm expecting him any day now. He'll

put the fear of God into Loomis, or my name's not Maddie O'Hara. Loomis'll learn to by-damn respect a lady!''

Actually, her real name wasn't Maddie O'Hara, but he didn't expect this was the time to bring it up. He dug into his pocket for the card, then pushed it across the tabletop to Maddie.

He asked, ''Would your gunfighter have been carrying this?''

Maddie looked at it, and her shoulders sank. ''Where'd you find it?''

''On the desert, a few miles out,'' Slocum said. ''He'd been dead about a week or so. Hard to tell. Coyotes had been at him.''

''Eew,'' said Charity.

''Why don't you just pack up and leave?'' he asked again, and this time Maddie listened.

Her eyed narrowed. Softly, and with great determination, she said, ''Because it's my land and I intend to keep it, Slocum. It's already been swiped from me once by Daddy O'Hara, and now that I've got it back, it's staying right in these two hands. It's the principle of the thing.''

Slocum lifted a brow. ''I hesitate to say it, Maddie, but I don't recall you being much on principle in the past.''

She didn't whack him over the head with a broken stool, as he half-expected she would. Instead, she said, quite calmly, ''That was an awfully long time ago, Slocum.''

"And I'm staying with Maddie," Charity announced. "She was good to me. Nobody else, besides Jane here, has ever been good to me. I mean, not without wanting something."

"Me too," said Jane. "The three musketeers."

"All for one and one for all, I guess." Maddie sighed.

Slocum remembered something. "What about Ann-Elizabeth?"

"Well, then," she said, pointedly ignoring him. "With Mr. Taylor murdered by that conniving skunk Loomis—"

"I didn't say he was murdered, Maddie," Slocum said carefully. "I just said he was dead. He could have fallen off his horse and cracked his skull on a rock, for all we know."

She sniffed, and he knew she didn't believe him. She didn't say so, though. She just said, "I guess it's up to you now."

4

"Leave, Maddie," Slocum said. It was late. Pedro was outside, standing the first watch—as well as he could, what with his hangover—and everyone else had turned in for the night.

She closed her eyes for a moment. "We've been through this before, Slocum. This is my land."

"And it's played out. Worthless."

Her full lips pursed for a moment, and he could tell that what she really wanted to do was haul off and slug him, but she only said, "Mine. It's round-about, but I own it."

"Through a father your mother was never married to," he said, gently. "Maddie, honey, the only thing that made this chunk of rock worth anything at all was the gold that was in it, and you've already dug out what Daddy O'Hara missed. There's no grassland, no water, no nothing. Hell, Daddy O'Hara wasn't even your real daddy, just a cheap con man with grandiose ideas."

"Cheap, *murdering* con man with grandiose ideas," she corrected him. "But the point is that he weaseled it out of my real father. And married to Mama or not, that makes it mine. I've got the paperwork. You know I do. You got it for me, Slocum, remember?''

He remembered. He sighed, weary of the argument, resigned to the fact that she wouldn't give in, not his Maddie. She was as stubborn as she was beautiful—and just as devious of mind—and he'd pulled her bacon out of the fire two years ago. But not before she'd baked up a ground-glass dessert for Daddy O'Hara and watched him die in agony.

The bastard had deserved that, and worse.

He figured that there was something she wasn't telling him—with Maddie, that would just be expected—and that nobody, not even he, would be able to pry it out of her until she was ready. So he took the path of least resistance, and changed the subject.

"Darlin'?" he said. "You want to tell me again why all you gals were bare-naked when I walked in here?''

She smiled. It was a welcome sight. "I told you, Slocum. We were distracting Mace.''

He said, "Well, now, I believe I could use a little distraction myself.''

Her smile went to a grin, and took on a decidedly ornery bent that had him suddenly—and unexpectedly—hard.

"Why, Mr. Slocum!" she said. "I'm positively shocked! A man of your upright stature!''

"Upright would be just the right word, darlin',''

he said, getting to his feet. He stood over her. "I don't reckon there's anyplace we could go to look into this problem, is there? Course, there's always that table over there, but it's all shot up and splintery."

"Not that you'd care," she said, brushing her palm over the straining front of his britches. She stood up, facing him, that ornery grin never leaving her face. "It wouldn't be *your* back getting porcupined. Course, it's been so long since I saw you last that I probably wouldn't mind."

She led him down the hallway to her room, where he shucked his clothes in record time, and then she made him sit on the bed while she undressed for him in the lantern light—slowly, teasingly.

"Just hold your horses, Slocum," she admonished when he tried to hurry her up. She wagged her finger at him and slithered out of yet another petticoat. "Just sit back against those pillows and watch the show. Go on, you stinker, get back."

By the time she was naked, he was more than ready, and when she sashayed close enough, he threw an arm around her and pulled her onto the bed. He had her legs spread wide before she hit the mattress.

"Slocum!" she said with a laugh as he centered himself over her. "I believe that next time, I'm going to have to tie you up!"

And then she gasped as he entered her, a gasp

of pleasure that was accompanied by a monumental buck of her hips. And Slocum, as much to his relief as his chagrin, came in a thunderous rush.

"Good Christ, Maddie!" he said, once he could breathe again. "I'm sorry. I'll make it up to you. But Lord, what with you parading around in your birthday suit first thing and then that show just now . . . well, it's been a long time."

"You act," she said, rolling him onto his back so that she was on top, "as if this show's closing for the night." She nibbled his ear, her full breasts rubbing pebbled nipples against his chest. "But cowboy," she whispered, "I'm here to tell you that it's just getting started."

Slocum smiled. "Is that right?"

She trailed her tongue down his neck, then across it and up to the other ear. Worrying the lobe between her teeth, she said, "A fact, Slocum. Whether you like it or not."

He ran his hands down her sides, over the indentation of her waist and the swell of her hips, to cup her fanny in both hands. It was as firm and as round as he remembered it, and he kneaded the flesh gently, running his middle fingers up and down the crease.

She whispered, "If you're trying to work me into a tizzy, darlin', you've got a good start on it." She brought her mouth over his. An inch from his lips, she murmured, "And I already had a head start. Began the second I saw you in my hallway."

She lowered her mouth to his then, and he kissed her deeply. Being with Maddie was like being home. She was comfortable and agreeable and warm, like a crackling hearth fire on a Georgia night in winter. But at the same time, he never knew what to expect of her. When it came to loving, she was a kitten mewling for cream one minute, and a catamount on the scent of game the next.

He just kept on kissing her, feeling the heat rise up in his loins as his fingers dipped lower, between her legs. When he felt her moisture on his fingertips, she groaned against his mouth and pushed down onto his hands.

"Already, baby?" she whispered hoarsely, still twisting against his fingers. "It hasn't even been five minutes."

"Shhh," he breathed.

He slid a finger within her, then two, and she let out a low moan and whispered, "God, Slocum. Just keep doing that."

He chuckled deep in his throat. "Just getting warmed up, darlin'."

And then she froze, went absolutely stock-still, and before he could begin to wonder what was wrong, she said, "Shit!" and climbed off him.

He reached for her, saying, "What?" But she was already throwing on a robe.

"Don't you hear it, Slocum?" she snapped as she cinched the belt. "He's back again!"

"Who?"

"Listen!"

He strained his ears, and then, faintly, he heard it: not the sound of gunfire, or of stealthy creeping, or even the distant whoops of an unlikely Indian attack. It was the sound of a quavering male voice, unaccompanied by anything that could have kept it on pitch, and the voice was singing "Lorena." Well, it thought it was "Lorena."

He laughed.

"It's that damn Mace Cantrell!" Maddie spat, ignoring his laughter and pulling his revolver from the pile of clothes he'd left on the floor. "He's back *again*!"

Stark naked and still grinning, Slocum leapt from the bed and stopped her. "Hold up!" he said, and wrested the gun from her hand. "You're not about to plug anybody with my gun just for singin' out of tune, Maddie."

She crossed her arms over her ample chest and snorted. "Then *you* take care of it."

"Anything to get you back in bed, Maddie," he said, and grabbed for his pants.

"Just for curiosity's sake, you mind telling me why I'm supposed to shoot this fella?" he asked as they crept along the darkened hallway. The off-kilter singing grew increasingly louder, and now he could hear Jane—at least, he thought it was Jane—moaning.

He was tempted to ask why anything that would

make Jane moan was necessarily a bad thing, but he held his tongue.

The moaning grew louder when they stopped in front of the first door off the hall, and louder still when Maddie opened the door. There was Jane, in bed, her fanny up in the air, and her hands clutching a pillow to her head.

"Jesus!" she cried when she saw them. "Make the caterwauling sonofabitch stop it!"

"Every other night, he's out there wailing," Maddie explained as she pushed Slocum toward the window. "Now, take care of it!"

Slocum would have thought that Jane was certainly capable of taking care of a little moonlight serenade—she'd impressed him as somebody who could take care of a cavalry charge single-handed—but he went to the window. Anything to keep Maddie happy.

He pulled back the curtains, and there stood Mace, eyes closed, head thrown back, singing his heart out. His hands were clasped before him, and there was a dollar bill clutched in them.

"The years slip slowly by, Lo-reeeeee-na," he wailed, *"the dew is on the frost again."*

Mace was rotten with melodies, but he was worse with lyrics.

"Hey!" called Slocum. "It's 'the snow is on the ground'!"

He didn't stick his head out the window, though. This gave every appearance of a simple serenade, but considering what had happened that afternoon, you never could tell when there'd be a few more fellows hiding in the bushes. With guns.

Mace opened his eyes. "Hey, you ain't Janie." He blinked. "You're that feller from this afternoon! Say, you shouldn't' spooked off our horses like that. It was three miles afore we caught 'em up! And what're you doin' in Jane's room anyhow?" he added with no small degree of umbrage. "I got my dollar right here! I can pay! My money's just as good as yours."

Slocum, who had by this time determined that Mace was alone, said, "Go home, you fool. There are people trying to sleep in here."

"Not till I get serviced! I got a dollar, I tell you!" he shouted, waving it. "I got a dollar and these gals got the goods. Why won't they barter like normal folks? Why they gotta go and stick a knife to a feller's privates till his bladder's about to commence, then tease him till his balls are blue? That Jane, she teased me bad, mister. You seen what she was doin' to me, sitting there nekkid as a jaybird with her legs goin' north an' south and all the time touchin' herself! Why won't she take my money?"

Slocum actually felt sorry for him for a second. After all, the poor fellow looked next to tears. But then Jane elbowed him aside. She leaned out the window, her heavy breasts straining the thin cotton of her nightgown.

"Mace Cantrell," she called, "I've had it with you and your goddamn tuneless warbling and your nothing-on-your-mind-but-your-pecker too! Get the hell out of here before I take it into my head to get the shotgun and blast you again!"

Again? Slocum thought.

But Mace just smiled dreamily. "You got fine titties, Jane, real fine. Beautiful. The best I ever seen."

"Thought you said you'd never seen a naked woman before," Maddie broke in.

Mace straightened. "They was the best ones in the whole room," he said defensively.

"Get!" Jane thundered. "Just get! I'm not in that business anymore, you hear?"

"But honey—" Mace began.

"Don't call me honey!" she shouted, grabbed the pistol from Slocum's hand, and put a slug into the dust at Mace's feet.

"Give that back!" said Slocum, and pulled the gun away from her.

"Janie!" wailed Mace.

"Well, he pisses me off," Jane grumbled. "And if you won't let me shoot him, the least you can do is get him out of here. And keep him out!"

5

Wearily, Slocum sat himself down on one of the few porch chairs that hadn't been damaged by the afternoon's gun battle. He kept his pistol in his lap—he wasn't ready to trust the cowhand yet—but motioned Mace into the chair across from him.

"Let's hear your side of it," he said, "and make it short." Maddie was waiting in the back bedroom, after all.

But Mace demanded, "Who are you, mister? Ed told us you said your name was Slocum, but that don't mean shit to me."

"Ed? Oh, yeah. The big tough guy with the busted razor blade."

"Ed's got sensitive skin, that's all," Mace replied defensively. "And who the hell are you to just ride in here, purty as you please, and hog all the whores for sixty miles?"

Slocum shrugged. "Nobody. Just an old friend of Maddie O'Hara's who happened to ride in."

Mace stood up again. "Well, then, I'll thank you kindly to just happen to ride out."

Slocum cocked his pistol. Mace stared at him. Slocum said, "I'd sit down again and act friendly, if I were you."

Mace sat.

"Now, I'm just tryin' to figure this thing out, Mace," Slocum said. "If you could give me a hand, I'd be appreciative."

The cowhand scowled, but he said, "What d'you want to know?"

"Lots of things," Slocum replied, "but most especially, I want to know why the hell these gals put up with you. Have you got any ideas? Far as I can tell, they could have just pulled up stakes any time and lit out."

Mace snorted. "That just shows you don't know much. Maddie ain't gonna leave her land, and the others are sworn to stand by her."

"Then why on earth is your boss convinced that if he throws her off her land, she'll be content to settle happily into his little gold-plated whorehouse? There's a whole wide world out there, and these gals could go anywhere in it. Three Wives isn't the whole dad-blamed universe. What's to keep them from just stepping on a stage and flashing their butts at you on the way out of town?"

This seemed to stump Mace, who sat scratching his chin. Slocum had guessed him at about twenty-two or twenty-three. Just a kid really. And not a very smart kid, judging by what he'd see so far.

"Well," Mace said finally, "they just wouldn't, that's all. Mr. Loomis says they won't. Mr. Loomis says he's got on 'em a legality. And Mr. Loomis, he's always right."

Slocum leaned back wearily. "Was he right when he sent you up here to shoot up this place? You can't bed a gal if she's shot dead."

"Well, Mrs. Loomis didn't rightly send us," Mace said. "Not direct-like. See, I was just thinkin' about Jane, you know? Thinking about her soft, pink skin and that little hollow at the base of her neck, and wonderin' what her toes looked like. And Mike—that's my little brother—he says, 'Why don't we just ride on over there and see them gals?' "

He paused for a moment, explaining, "My brother Mike, he's kinda soft on the one they call Charity."

Slocum nodded.

"And we get to talkin' about it, and Ed, he says, 'This tack can get mended just as well tomorrow as today,' and then some'a the other boys said sure, that sounded great, and—"

Slocum held up a hand. "The shooting?"

Sheepishly, Mace said, "Ed gets kinda mad sometimes. And I guess we was all worked up some. When them gals turned us down, wouldn't even listen to us even though we had seven dollars cash between us? When that Maddie O'Hara come at us with a rifle and Jane with a shotgun? Well, old Ed, he just went kinda crazy, you know? I guess the rest of us followed along."

"And Carl Loomis didn't have anything to do with it?"

"No, sir," Mace said, shaking his head. "Other than that he said we could all go, and gave us five dollars, not a blamed thing."

Slocum sighed and shook his head. "You just think a spell on that, Mace. I can tell you right now that Loomis is dead wrong. He was dead wrong to send you over here with money, and he's dead wrong about these gals moving to his whorehouse. They're tough. They're not going to do what he says—or any man says—just because he says it. Weren't they blasting back at you when I rode up today? Didn't they wing one of your boys?"

"My brother," Mace allowed. "Just hit the meat." He dipped fingers into his shirt pocket, and brought out the greenback again. He handed it toward Slocum. "Please, mister?"

"Slocum."

"All right. Please, Slocum, then," he said. "I just gotta have that Jane gal. She's about to drive me wild! I can't stop thinkin' about her, about that honey-blond hair and them big tits and the way she sashays in the be-hind! Hellfire and brimstone! You seen her, Slocum! I'll go crazy if I don't have her! Ain't a dollar enough? If it's more they want, I got it!"

Slocum watched as he dug out another wadded dollar bill and carefully straightened it on his knee.

He held it out too. "See?"

Slocum half-wished that Jane would take pity

on the boy, if only so that *he* could get back to Maddie. But he said, "The lady just plain isn't interested, Mace."

And then he had an idea. Loomis's crew had shot the place up pretty good this afternoon. They'd turned Maddie's home, which had been a fine frame rambler of a ranch house, with furnishings well above the average, into a demolition area.

"You know, Mace," Slocum began thoughtfully, "you can catch more flies with honey than you can with lead slugs."

Mace's face twisted on the darkened porch. "Huh?"

"Ever stop to think," he said, "that these ladies might have quit the whoring game, but that don't necessarily mean they ain't interested in the opposite sex."

Mace stared at him.

"What I mean to say," Slocum continued, "is that maybe they don't want your money. Haven't they turned it down enough times to convince you of that?"

"So many times my pockets is frayed from takin' it in and out! But—"

Slocum cut him off. "Well, in my experience, when a lady says no, she means no. Likewise, when she says yes, she means that too."

"I don't know about that," Mace said with all

seriousness. "I was always told they was contrary as mules."

"You act like they're a different species, Mace," Slocum said, although he was half-convinced of it himself. "Why, they're just people. Practically just like you and me, except for a few notable physical differences."

That didn't come out right, and he added, "Well, a few differences up here too." He tapped his head.

Mace made a face.

"A lady likes to be wooed and cajoled, not bought and paid for, Mace," Slocum said with a sigh. "Unless, of course, it's her line of work, which it ain't anymore for these gals."

Mace shook his head. "You wanna get to the point?"

"Fix the house, Mace," Slocum said, and stood up. Maddie was waiting. "Get your backside over here and fix up the damage you idiots did to their house and their furniture. And be nice to Jane. Real nice. No more flashing cash around. Sweet-talk her, and do for her. You follow?"

"Sweet-talk?"

"That's right."

"Like a church gal?"

"Exactly like it."

"Aw, cripes." Mace stood up too, and started for the front door.

"Christ," Slocum muttered, and caught him by

the shoulder. "Tomorrow's plenty soon enough, don't you think? Now, go home."

After he watched Mace ride off, Slocum went in search of Pedro, who was supposedly on guard. He found him curled up in a stall in the barn, hugging the empty mescal bottle.

Slocum kicked at his boot, and when that didn't rouse him, he shouted, "Pedro!"

There was no reply, and finally Slocum just walked back up to the house. After talking to Mace, he figured that for tonight, at least, they weren't in any imminent danger—and probably in no great need of a guard—but still, he planned to have a little talk with Pedro the next morning.

He let himself into the house, and began to feel his way down the hall, thinking all the while. It was a squirrely setup, all right. Nobody's story held water, so far as he could tell. What he needed to do was to talk to Loomis—or at least take a look at him—but right at the moment, he had an overpowering urge to locate Maddie's room.

Sure enough, there was a golden fan of light showing beneath her door. She'd waited for him.

He found her sitting cross-legged on the bed and rolling herself a smoke. From his fixings, it looked like.

"You send that single-minded little sex fiend home to Jesus?" she asked, keeping her eyes on her fingers—and the quirlie she was rolling.

"What'd you do, Slocum, strangle him? I didn't hear so much as a shot."

He shucked out of his britches. "Nope. Sent him home to bed."

"What kind of guardian angel are you anyhow?" She gave the smoke a last lick, and without looking his way, held out a hand. "Hand me a sulphur-tip, would you?"

Grinning, he walked over and rested his erect cock across her palm.

She still didn't turn all the way toward him, but he could see enough of her face to tell that that ornery look had taken hold of her features again.

"That's an awful big lucifer you've got there, cowboy," she said, lips curled into a bow. "Take a lot of rubbing to get that one to burst into flame."

"Oh," he said, "not so much as you might think."

With two fingers, she flipped her unlit smoke across the room. "Maybe you're right. Appears to me to be already half-lit."

"Fair to smolderin'," he said.

Her fingers curled around his cock, and she pulled it—with him following directly—onto the mattress, saying, "C'mon, cowboy. Let's light this bonfire."

6

The next morning, Slocum was up before any of the women. He grabbed a couple of chicken legs from the platter on the counter, and chewing, headed down toward the barn and the corral and his mare.

While Geraldo lounged against a fence pole, watching, he tacked her up. The Mexican was a lean fellow and tall, with a drooping mustache, a touch of gray at the temples, and a set of crooked but very white teeth. The bandage that the girls had wrapped his head with yesterday had been discarded in favor of a flamboyant sombrero, which he wore low on his forehead.

Much altered from last night's drunken buffoonery, he looked as though he had the potential to be a most deadly fellow.

"Where you been blasting, Geraldo?" Slocum asked casually. He reached under the mare's belly for the girth strap. "Back in the days when you used to find color, that is."

"Over that hill," Geraldo answered lazily, and pointed to the north.

He was obviously hungover, a condition that

most likely hadn't been improved by standing guard the last half of the night. Of course, Slocum doubted he'd actually stood much of it. Short, squat Pedro had supposedly been on duty earlier, and that hadn't kept Mace Cantrell from wandering in and screeching out six mangled-lyrics choruses of "Lorena" without rousing him. Slocum decided that the first thing after he got back, he'd do a hunt for the Who-Hit-John.

"Can you show me the place?" Slocum asked. He snugged the girth, then waited for Bess to let out her breath so he could tighten it one more notch.

Geraldo gave him a pained look. "Now? You want I should show you this morning?" His hangover must have been worse than it looked.

Bess exhaled with a loud snort, and Slocum gave the latigo a last tug. "Yup," he said.

"*Mierda,*" mumbled the Mexican, but he saddled a tall sorrel gelding anyway, and twenty minutes later he and Slocum were riding out through the brush and gradually putting the ranch house and its cluster of buildings behind them.

By way of conversation, Geraldo said, "Your mare, she is a nice one."

"Thanks," said Slocum. "Traded a stud horse for her up in Montana."

Geraldo nodded, then said, "How come you know Señorita Maddie O'Hara so well that you make the screwing all night?"

The question took Slocum by surprise, and he raised a brow. "Can't hardly see that it's any of your business, Geraldo, unless you've got some sort of claim on her yourself."

The Mexican hurriedly shook his head. "No, Señor, no," he said, holding up a hand. "I am just curious. The ladies, they don't like men very much, I don't think. Oh, they are very nice with Pedro and me. Very polite, so long as we stay in the barn at night. But every man who is not in their employ gets a double-barreled greeting, *comprende*? I just wondered why you did not."

It was a fair question. Slocum supposed it must seem odd to see women who'd been shooting first and asking questions later welcome him with open arms. Among other appendages.

He decided to keep it simple. "Well, I first ran into Maddie a couple of years back. Her 'daddy' kicked up a bit of a fracas down south and I got tangled up in it. That's when I met Maddie."

Geraldo nodded, and reined his horse around a big clump of jumping cholla, giving it wide berth. "I have heard about Señor O'Hara a little bit from my cousin, who worked for him. He was no good, if you do not mind my saying so. He was not her real papa?"

"No," he said. "Her real daddy was a man named Sewell. She never knew him. He had this place for years without ever knowing there was gold in it. When he died, O'Hara just sort of took over running things. Claim-jumped it, in a manner of speakin'. Then he tracked down Maddie and brought her out here and tried to convince her to marry his son. Tryin' to sew up loose ends, I guess, legalize his hold on the land. Reckon Maddie keeps the O'Hara name just cause she's used to it.''

"I am glad to hear that, Señor. I am thinking this is the case, but it is good to hear it for sure.''

"Call me Slocum.''

"*Sí.*''

The meandering trail that they followed swung downward into a small gorge, and Geraldo reined in his sorrel just before the trail turned downward, under the shade of an immense ironwood tree. "Here, Slocum,'' he said, pointing. "Here is where we blasted, and Señor Daddy O'Hara before us, or so I am told.''

Down they went, and as they neared the place, Slocum took silent inventory.

There had sure enough been men working here, and long enough to do a good bit of damage to the landscape. The walls of the gorge were pockmarked by blast holes, and some of the larger—and he assumed, more productive—holes had been framed up with timber. Rusty narrow-gauge rails ran down the center of the gorge. A small rail wagon lay in the weeds beside the track, tipped on its side, and a gecko sunbathing there flicked its tail at him.

"Well, nobody's worked here for a good bit," Slocum observed. They were down on the floor of the gorge by this time.

"Not for maybe a year," Geraldo said. "The gold, she is all used up."

"They ever prospect anyplace else?"

Geraldo shrugged his shoulders. "Who knows? Señorita Maddie O'Hara, she say this was the only place of the gold."

Slocum was beginning to believe that the whole crew was about two bricks shy of a load. Any fool with half a grain of sense and the curiosity God gave him would have ranged out, followed the line of the vein, even if there wasn't any gold showing. Veins as rich as this one sometimes stopped suddenly, only to pick up miles away.

Well, sometimes.

Had Maddie bothered to look, or was everybody around here as lackadaisical as Geraldo?

He decided to set that thought on the back burner, and said, "Which way to town?"

Geraldo pointed. "Four miles from here. You want me to ride to town with you?" His expression was pained. He probably wanted to crawl back into bed with that hangover.

Slocum didn't answer. Instead, he asked, "And which way to the Loomis spread?"

Geraldo hesitated. "Is not a good idea to go there, Slocum."

"Didn't say I was goin'. Just wanted to know which way."

Geraldo shrugged and pointed in the other direction. "Two miles from here, three from the house. Don't go, okay? The ladies, they have a friend in you. Why you want to go getting killed so quick? Why you want to leave them alone?"

Slocum dug into his pocket for his fixings. "Got no intention of getting myself killed, Geraldo." He sprinkled tobacco into the paper, rolled it, and gave it a quick lick. "You ever hear of an hombre named Grant Taylor?"

"*Sí!*" came the reply. "This is the man Señorita Maddie hires to come here." His dark brow furrowed. "But yesterday . . . Did not you say you find him on the desert?"

Slocum flicked a lucifer into life and held it to his smoke. "Just checkin' to see if you were paying attention, Geraldo," he said with a smile.

"No, I think you check to see how smart I am, Slocum," Geraldo said, and Slocum nearly choked on a lungful of smoke. "I think you think that me and Pablo are two dumb Mexicanos. Well, you listen to this, Señor Slocum, and listen good. The ladies, they have been good to us."

Slocum opened his mouth to say something, but Geraldo wasn't finished yet.

"They hire us to dig the gold when nobody else would hire Mexicans—or trust us—and they work right alongside us, and keep us on after all the gold

is gone. They treat us fine and the food is good,
like that chicken you were putting away when you
come down to saddle your mare. So we will stick
with them, no matter how crazy they act, for as
long as they will have us."

"Beg your pardon, Geraldo," Slocum said—a
little hoarsely, on account of the swallowed smoke
still being rough in his lungs. "The ladies seem to
have inspired quite a loyalty in you boys. Didn't
mean to get you riled."

Geraldo seemed to relax in his saddle, and Slocum assumed his apology had been accepted.
"Slocum, what the ladies were back in the East
does not matter to Pablo and me. What matters is
that they are here now. Everybody, he starts out
one thing and becomes another, *comprende*?"

"*Es verdad,*" Slocum said with a nod. "Hell,
I've been everything in the book and a few things
besides." He took a long drag on his cigarette.
"Bet you have too."

"*Sí,*" was all Geraldo said, and although Slocum was hoping for a more detailed answer, he
didn't press the issue.

The Mexican gathered his reins. "You need me
for more of the sightseeing, or can I go back?"

Slocum's mouth crooked up. He said, "No, you
go on your way. Thanks, Geraldo."

"*Por nada,*" Geraldo said, and reined his horse
back the way they'd come. Slocum watched him
go, climbing up the side of the gorge with that big

sombrero stiffly flapping in the wind. When he reached the tableland and the big ironwood tree at the top, he turned his horse back for a moment.

"Hey, Slocum?" he shouted down. "Be careful of that Ed Barlow. He is bad business."

Maddie looked over the wrinkled paper for the second time, her fingers crushing the edges as her hands fisted on the page.

"Hellfire and damnation!" she said again.

"They're crazy!" said Charity, who was hanging over her shoulder.

"What!" demanded Jane. "Somebody tell me what's going on!"

"If you'd let us teach you how to read—" Charity began, but Jane cut her off.

"Gone all my life without it just fine," she said. "Don't see any point in cramming more nonsense into my brain at this late date."

"Oh," said Charity, propping her fists on her hips. "And a whorehouse in Chicago is doing just fine."

"Reading didn't keep you out of the life, now did it, sugar plum?" Jane answered too sweetly.

Charity took a step toward her. "I could just snatch you bald sometimes, Jane!"

Maddie flung her arm back, cutting off Charity's path. "Christ!" she growled, her eyes still directed at the paper before her. "Could we worry about that later?"

She flicked her eyes toward Jane, who crossed her arms and said, "I'd ask again what's on the paper, but certain people are getting downright snappish with me."

Maddie ignored Jane's tone, as well as the little push Charity gave to her arm. She said, "It's an eviction notice, that's what it is. Ward Semple rode out here and threw an eviction notice at me, wrapped around a rock. Some sheriff, afraid to come to the door. The cowardly sonofabitch!"

"What?" exclaimed Jane, moving quickly to the table and snatching the crumpled paper. She peered at it, holding it upside down. "They can't evict you, Maddie! You said this place was yours, free and clear! Just because some old fool—"

"It is," she said. "My daddy paid it off twenty years ago. My real daddy, that is."

"Well, then," said Charity, brushing her skirts dismissively. "That's that then. Who wants to help me glue these plates back together?"

Maddie sighed. Charity was sweet, but sometimes she could be dense—particularly when she didn't want to face something.

"No," Maddie said patiently, "that isn't that. Seems that Carl Loomis finally decided to stick it to us. He's charging us for the water. He wants to charge us going back twenty years, as a matter of fact, and he's got Whit Cramer on his side."

"That's plain foolish!" Jane roared. "Can't he see he's gone round the bend? Lead me to that bastard! I'll show him water rights! If he's still trying to force us into that whorehouse of his to pay off his stupid bill, he's plumb crazy.''

Maddie closed her eyes. *I wish Slocum hadn't gone off meandering this morning,* she thought. *Just like a man to go wandering off on some damn fool errand when you need him.*

''I don't know if it's crazy or not, Jane,'' she said, and her level tone ‘surprised her. Well, she supposed somebody had to be the voice of reason. It had been, by turns, Jane or Charity or herself these past few months. It could have been Ann-Elizabeth too, if the silly girl hadn't turned tail and just ridden off in Maddie's buckboard one day. Funny. Maddie'd always thought Ann-Elizabeth was the most sensible of any of them.

''I want to talk to Slocum about it,'' Maddie continued, ''before any one of us goes off half-cocked. This isn't Chicago. You never can tell what old laws they've got on the books out here. But listen—if Loomis really has got us—I mean, if he can really make this water thing stick—then I want you girls to take off like Ann-Elizabeth did.''

Jane flicked her the evil eye, and Maddie added hastily, ''Well, you know what I mean. Just leave, no fanfare. There's to be no staying around on my behalf, and I mean that.''

Charity said, ''Now, Maddie . . .''

''No,'' said Maddie. ''I mean it. The sonofabitch may have his hooks into me, but he's got no claims on you gals." Again, she looked at the paper in her hands. "That damn Loomis has tried about everything else to get us off this place, short of burning it down."

Charity gasped, and whispered, "Don't say that, Maddie! Don't give him any ideas!"

Jane rolled her eyes, but gave Charity's shoulders a little hug.

"I swear to God," Maddie continued in a low tone, "if we ever see the light at the other end of this tunnel, I'm going to run my sheep right up Loomis's butt."

Jane's attention snapped to the window. "Somebody's coming," she said. She went to it and squinted through the spikes of broken glass. "It's that Mace Cantrell!" she announced angrily, adding, "Riding up here in broad daylight all by himself, and big as you please!"

"Mace?" Maddie couldn't figure out for the life of her what in the world would make him so bold. They'd already filled him full of bird shot two times when he'd come at night, and in the daylight he'd make a much better target.

"Where'd you put that greener, Maddie?" Jane asked, then spied it and snatched it down off its hooks. Charity was already in the corner, ducked down and curled up like a Texas armadillo.

Maddie came out of her chair so quickly that she knocked it over. Just in time, she shoved the shotgun's barrel away from the window.

"Just hold on, Jane!" she said sternly. "He's alone, and it's right in the middle of the day, like you said. Don't you think maybe he has something important to tell us? What else would convince him to come up here and make such a good target?"

Jane scowled, but she let the shotgun hang, nose down. "All right," she allowed. "But if he's set on any funny business, or any of that singing bullshit, remember—this time, I'm the one who gets to shoot him."

Like you didn't shoot him both times before? Maddie thought, but she patted Jane's arm. "That's right, dear."

Mace knocked on the door, and after taking time for one deep breath, Maddie opened it.

"Yes?" she said sweetly. Acting had always been her strong suit.

Mace, who appeared to be taken aback by the civil greeting, stuttered for a moment, then wordlessly swept his hat off his head. "M-ma'am?" he said.

Maddie peered at him. "Yes?"

He swallowed and tried to look past her, into the house.

Maddie tried again. Much more of this, and she'd give Jane leave to start blasting. "What it is, Mace?" she said slowly. "You leave something behind when we de-pants'd you yesterday?"

There were giggles from inside the house. Mace turned bright red, and for moment she nearly felt sorry for him. That was, until she remembered his swagger when he'd burst in on them the day before, making demands.

"I-I seen you gals naked too," he said in weak defense.

"So has most of Illinois and half of Michigan," Maddie replied. She'd lost her taste for niceties. "Get on with it, Mace, or get ready to catch another load of bird shot."

"No, no!" he said hurriedly, holding up his hand. "You don't know how that pains a fella when they go to dig it out. Mr. Slocum sent me."

"I knew it!" said Jane's voice, from behind her. "Men! They're all in it together!"

Maddie snapped, "Quiet, Jane!" then said, "Mace, what are you talking about? Is he hurt? What's wrong?"

His fingers were working the brim of his hat with gusto now. "Ain't hurt, ma'am. It's just that last night, he told me I'd better come help you clean up the mess we done made. When we shot your place up, I mean."

Maddie tucked her chin in consternation. Mace must have see the confusion on her face, because he added, "Ain't no glass to be got right now. I checked in town. But I brung a hammer and nails. Thought maybe today I'd fix up them window frames for you."

7

Three Wives wasn't much of a town.

A mercantile and Three Wives Dry Goods, a barbershop (which also advertised undertaker's services), the small City Hall and tiny jail, the Cattlemen's First Bank, and two saloons seemed to be the main staples. Smaller shops—a hardware, a tobacco shop, and three restaurants among them—filled the spaces in between on the three short streets that faced a dusty town square with a dustier bandstand.

On the fourth street, the street that completed the square, sat Three Wives' famous vacant whorehouse, in which Maddie and her friends were expected to take up residence.

It was so brand-new, Slocum thought, that you could practically still smell the paint. Two stories of mostly bright pink, with baby-blue and soft-purple and mustard-yellow trim, it had a turret and a wraparound porch and (as reported by Jane) machine-turned gingerbread galore.

It sat dead center in a wide, but very shallow, lot. There were extensive gardens—well, cactus gardens anyway—on either side, but only about six feet of land in front, to the street, and perhaps ten behind, to the alley.

Slocum figured the planning commissioner who'd come up with that setup was probably still drunk, or else in an insane asylum someplace. The bordello was more than the focus of the square. With the greenery on each side stretching out to take up the entire length of the street, and that big, busy Easter egg of a house planted smack dab in the center of it, it looked like the whole remainder of the town had been set up to pay it homage.

And considering Three Wives' population of women (or rather, lack thereof), maybe it had.

He made a slow circuit of the town square, then tied Bess in front of the Peeved Rooster saloon and walked through the swinging doors. The place was deserted, save for a balding barkeep lazily polishing glasses.

"Howdy," said the barkeep.

Slocum nodded. "Likewise. Beer."

When the bartender brought him his schooner, he took a sip, wiped the foam off his upper lip, and said, "Helluva name this place has got."

The barkeep smiled. "Three Wives, you mean, or the Peeved Rooster?"

Slocum smiled back. "Both, I reckon."

"Three Wives," the bartender said conversationally, as if he'd explained this many times before, "is because old Ezra Tate, the feller that founded our fair city, had him three squaw-wives all at once. Most people think it was cause he was Mormon, but they wasn't invented yet, I don't think."

Slocum sipped his beer. "A man ahead of his time. And the Peeved Rooster?"

The barkeep shrugged. "Tommy Waylon used to own it and he probably knew why he named it, but he got himself shot by a drunk Swede about ten years back. Nobody remembers now what the reason was. Spend quite a bit of my time tryin' to reason it out, when things get slow."

"Like they are now," Slocum said.

"Like they were till you walked in. Practically a rush. You just passin' through, or can I count on some return business?"

"Oh, I reckon I'll be back," Slocum said. He slung one elbow on the bar top and leaned on it, poking his thumb toward the door. "That's quite a whorehouse you got over there. When's the grand opening? All the sign says is 'soon.' "

The bartender snorted. "Said 'soon' for nigh on to two months, and the building's set vacant for nigh on six."

He picked up a shot glass and began to rub it vigorously, although to Slocum it looked as though he'd already polished it so many times that he was about to rub the fancy cut edges right off it.

"You got business in town, or you just passin'

through?'' the barkeep said, his eyes on the shot glass.

"Reckon it's both," Slocum replied. "Can I have a refill on this beer?"

"Well," the barkeep said as he drew a new one, " 'bout the only place to stay is over at the Widow Hubbard's. That'd be up over the mercantile."

Slocum remembered the name. Was she the bald woman, or the seventy-two-year-old?

He said, "Already staying with friends outside of town. Out at the O'Hara place."

Slocum's beer glass slipped from the barkeep's hands and smashed on the floor, sending up a gush of beer and foam.

Slocum stared at the froth dripping from the bartender's pants cuffs and boots. He said, "I guess you know the place?"

By the time Slocum left town and started back toward Maddie O'Hara's ranch, he'd been to the bank, the mercantile, and the general store, but no one had provided much in the way of usable information.

And everyone he'd talked to had evinced roughly the same reaction as the bartender.

It was beginning to irritate him.

Now, he could have understood if folks held sort of a grudge against Maddie. Orphaned at a young age and never having known her father, she had been resourceful enough and pretty enough (and amoral enough) to end up in a high-toned Chicago whorehouse, the sort that catered to the whims of the wealthy and influential.

When Daddy O'Hara turned up in the big city, and swept her home to his ranch, who could have blamed her for going with him? After all, she hadn't known that he'd paid a doctor to tell her she had tuberculosis and that the Arizona Territory was the place where she should recuperate. O'Hara hadn't told her that the ranch he was taking her to was rightfully the property of her late father. And he also hadn't told her that he planned to marry her off to his son, and cement the legalities, so that he could continue to mine her land for the gold with which he planned to start his lunatic empire.

He hadn't told her he was mad.

All in all, however, the considerable crew employed by Daddy O'Hara had practically kept the town of Three Wives in business. When Slocum and Maddie, with the aid of the U.S. Cavalry, had crushed O'Hara's plans, he'd supposed that they'd written a death sentence for the town of Three Wives as well.

Of course, he hadn't known about Loomis, and his considerable wealth.

Slocum's doing away with Daddy O'Hara didn't explain the townspeople's reaction to the mention of Maddie's name, nor did it do anything to explain Loomis's motivation for wanting them off the ranch. Which reminded him that he hadn't seen one steer, cow, or bull all day.

Now, that was passing strange. Maddie had told him that Loomis was a big rancher, head of the County Cattlemen's Association. You'd think a cattleman would have a cow or two.

Well, maybe they'd ranged out the other way, he reasoned. Maybe he'd pushed them up into the high country, where the grazing was better.

His hat flew off his head before he heard the rifle blast.

He dived off Bess, swatting her on the rump and scrambling into the brush, his own rifle pulled from the boot—and in his hand—without thinking. His hat had flown south, so he looked north, but he couldn't see a blessed thing. Any smoke the shot had discharged had fluttered away on the afternoon breeze long before he looked.

"Shit," he muttered, searching the distance. "Where the hell are you, you backshooting son-ofabitch?"

A second shot splintered the branch beside him and answered his question: Halfway up a small rise, a reflection of sun on rifle barrel gleamed for just a moment.

He returned fire immediately, but immediately was too late. A few seconds later, he watched a puff of dust—wrapped around a pony and a rider, no doubt—move rapidly from the base of the hill and disappear into the distance.

He stood up and retrieved his hat. Two holes—an entry and an exit hole, both big enough to stick his little finger through—marred the crown.

"Shit," he repeated, dusting it angrily on his pants.

All he'd wanted when he rode out here was to see Maddie again—and not incidently get himself a real quality lay—but so far he'd buried a stranger, walked into a houseful of naked women about to geld some addlepated cowpoke, dickered with an angry mob of men, and now somebody was shooting at him.

And they'd ruined a perfectly good hat.

He began to follow Bess's trail, cursing softly all the while.

8

Mace Cantrell met him on the road.

"Hey, Slocum!" he called from atop his chestnut as he rode forward. "The ladies are gonna be real pleased to see that you ain't dead! What'd you do, fall off'n your mare?"

Slocum just stared at him. If he hadn't been so tired, he would have pulled Mace off his damn pony and pounded him a few times.

But Mace stepped down all by himself, and offered a canteen. "Your mare come in all by her lonesome," he explained while Slocum drank. "Miss Maddie, she done sent me to find you."

Slocum wiped his mouth, then handed the canteen back. "*Miss* Maddie? That's some change from 'them whores.' "

Mace had the grace to blush. "I done what you said, Slocum. Went up there and offered to fix things, real friendly-like. Why, them women's fair nice, once you gets to know 'em."

"Yeah." Slocum ran his sleeve across his forehead, and it came away soaked. "They walk and talk just like real people."

"Yeah! They—" Mace stopped, scowling. "You funnin' with me?"

"Never had the thought," he said, eyeing Mace's gelding. It wasn't lathered, and whoever had taken that shot at him and then galloped away would have had a wet horse, even this long after the fact. Mace was in the clear, at least for the shooting.

"Mind?" Slocum said, stepping up on the chestnut before Mace had a chance to answer. He reined the horse around, then cleared the left stirrup of boot and stuck his hand down. "My walkin' muscles ain't what they used to be."

"I hear that," Mace replied, and climbed up to sit in back of him. "Just take him slow. Dimples ain't used to ridin' double."

Dimples? thought Slocum.

"Say," Mace went on as Slocum urged the chestnut into a walk, back toward Maddie's, "that appy a'yourn is sure a pretty thing. Lots a'muscle, but real fine in the head. Pretty blanket too. You lookin' to sell her?"

"Nope," said Slocum. He turned his head. "You put her up right, didn't you? Walked her out good and rubbed her down?"

"Miss Maddie was seein' to it when she sent me off," he answered. "Said you'd have all our guts for garters if your horse didn't get took care of right and proper."

Slocum nodded. He should have known Maddie would see to it. Good girl. He said, "Guess you got the day off from Loomis, if you came over here.''

''Sorta,'' came the sheepish reply.

''Well, did anybody else sorta get the day off?''

Behind him, he felt a movement as Mace shrugged. ''I dunno. Why?''

''Because somebody with a little too much free time on his hands took a couple potshots at me.''

Mace stiffened. ''It wasn't me, Slocum, I swear! I was fixin' the windersills for Miss Jane.'' Then his voice went dreamy. ''She's real picky about her windersills, that one. Likes 'em just so, and if'n you don't get 'em right, she give you a little swat on the back of the neck.''

He sighed. ''Gosh, she's purty, ain't she? She made me some limeade, and she even by-God strained out the seeds. Best limeade I ever tasted, bar none.''

Slocum rolled his eyes heavenward. ''No, I know it wasn't you shooting at me, Mace. What was your buddy Ed Barlow up to today?''

''Ed?'' Mace said. ''He ain't my buddy, no, sir. But he was tyin' down a bronc when I left. Reckon he was workin' broom-tails most of the day, cause we just brought in 'bout a dozen off the range. Real wild ones. Why? You think maybe old Ed was the feller what sighted down on you?''

''Hard to tell, Mace,'' Slocum said thoughtfully. ''Hard to tell.''

• • •

Slocum rocked his chair back on two legs and puffed on a most excellent cigar while he watched the women clear up the supper dishes. Charity was in her usual dither, but Jane was humming.

Jane worried him. She didn't hum with any degree of pleasantness, although her mouth was curled into a smile. The smile was, in fact, the thing that was bothering him. It was the smile of a cruel boy, one who's planning to torture a small animal later on, and is working out ways to draw it out, to increase the suffering.

Maddie appeared at his side and said, "Chair down, please?"

He obliged her by rocking it forward onto all four legs, and she obliged him by settling into his lap. She took the cigar from his fingers and puffed on it, blowing a perfect series of small smoke rings before she handed it back.

"Cuban," she said, putting his hand on her thigh. "The last box of Daddy O'Hara's stash."

He twisted the cigar in his fingers. "Why'd you keep the name O'Hara, Maddie?" he asked, although he was fairly certain he knew the answer. "I thought you hated the fat bastard."

She shrugged, a motion that rubbed one firm, cloth-covered breast against his chest. *Later,* he promised his awakening loins.

"It was just easier, that's all," she said, confirming his suspicions. "When everybody's been used to calling you O'Hara for two years, it's a bitch of a thing to switch them over to calling you Sewell. Besides, O'Hara wasn't his real moniker either, the stinking old pirate. Figured it was up for grabs.''

''Folks in town don't seem to want to hear about you in any case,'' he said. He rolled the cigar ash off against a small dessert plate Maddie'd left on the table for that purpose. ''All I got all day was spilled beer and dropped brooms and blinds set afire.''

''What?''

He smiled a little. ''Over at the bank. Mentioned your name, and the manager swung his cigar into the pull-blind. Caused quite a bit of excitement.''

She rested her head on his shoulder. ''You don't say.''

''Maddie, what in the name of U.S. Grant did you *do* to them?''

Her head came up and she jumped off his lap. ''John Slocum! I didn't do a blessed thing except offer to bring a little more prosperity to their piss-ant little town, and that's the truth, and if you have any thoughts otherwise, you can—''

''Hold it! Hold it!'' he soothed. He reached for her and caught her around the hips and hung on. ''I didn't mean—''

''Well, we didn't!'' said Charity, who had heretofore been occupied with gluing a broken cup back together. ''All we did was try to buy some sheep. And now they're so mean to us! The last time I went to town, nobody'd even wait on me! You'd think we had a disease or something!''

"We do have a disease, sweetie," Jane broke in. She turned from the pan of dishes she was washing, and said, "It's called ex-whore-itis. This rotten town's full of two-faced prigs—they want their whores, all right, but they want them in their place, which is underfoot and in town, where they can toss rocks at 'em when they're not screwing 'em.''

"So, leave Three Wives," Slocum said. Maybe they hadn't really heard him the first dozen times. Women could be like that.

But these women weren't.

"No," said Maddie.

"No," said Jane and Charity.

"Christ, you're stubborn," Slocum said under his breath.

"Thank you," Maddie said with a primly satisfied smile, then bumped his shoulder with her hip. "But you knew that, Slocum. You've always known that.''

Yes, he had. But that didn't mean he had to accept their explanation for what was going on in town.

If you asked him—which nobody seemed to be doing—the townsfolk gave the distinct impression of people who'd been threatened, not people who were on a witch-hunt for errant whores, or who were cranky because their local brothel was going vacant.

But he didn't want to start the three of them going. He'd wait until he had Maddie alone to voice any opinions he might have.

"Mace did a nice job on the windowsills," he said, "considering he didn't have much lumber to work with, that is."

Charity looked up from her teacup. "He did the chairs too. He's pretty sweet, when he isn't singing the paint off the outside of the house at two in the morning."

"I was surprised," Maddie said, nodding her head. "And you sending him? Slocum, will your matchmaking never end?"

He swatted at her bottom, but she danced out of his grasp too fast, and all he caught was the fabric of her skirt.

"Matchmaking, my ass," he grumbled around his cigar. "I just figured that if you kept him busy pounding nails and sawing wood all day, he'd be too tired to do anything but sleep come night. That's all."

"And you had nothing to do with those calf-eyes he was making at Jane all day long?" Maddie teased.

"Not a thing," he growled. "You know the story about the old coot who founded the town?"

Maddie nodded.

"Well, I was just thinkin' that he probably died

a young man, what with three women buzzing around all the goddamn time, correctin' and accusin' him and callin' him names.''

Maddie raised her brow. "Names?"

"Matchmaker, for starters," he said. "Old Ezra Tate probably killed himself. Probably wrote a note that said 'I quit' and hanged himself from a goddamn barn rafter."

Charity snickered into her teacup, but Maddie laughed right out loud and grabbed his arm and pulled him to his feet.

"What!" he half-shouted, in the spirit of the thing. "Haven't I suffered enough at the hands of you three women? I've got a hole clean through the brim of my new Stetson, and—"

"You've had that same old hat for as long as I've known you," Maddie broke in, laughing.

"That's not even two years," he said indignantly. "That's practically brand-new, for a hat."

"Well," she said, wrapping her arms around him and moving to a tune only she could hear, "you can buy a new one in Vista Verde."

He'd started box-stepping with her, but he stopped before he hit the count of four. "Why should I go to Vista Verde. I just got here!"

"But you are," she said. "You're going tomorrow, to pick up my sheep."

"Maddie, you're crazy." He pulled her hands away from his middle and held her out at arm's length. "I need to stick close by and keep an eye on things. There are people out there shooting at you, and—"

"No," she corrected him, "shooting at *you*."

"Well, they probably figure it's the same thing," he said. "Now ain't the time for me to leave you and go ridin' off, just as pretty as you please, for a load of sheep."

"It's called a flock," Charity said. She'd finished gluing the last teacup. "A herd of cattle, a flock of sheep, a gaggle of geese, a murder of crows, an exultation of larks, a clutch of—"

"A murder of crows?" Slocum broke in.

Charity shrugged her narrow shoulders. "I think so anyhow."

"I like that one," Jane said, wiping her hands on a dishtowel. "That's nice, Charity. The lark thing too."

"It'll just take a couple of days, Slocum," Maddie continued. "We've got Mace coming to court Jane and mend the house during the days, and Pedro and Geraldo to watch over us during the night."

"Some help they'll be," he muttered.

"Yes, they will," Maddie insisted. "Last night they were drunk as a couple of skunks and shot up to boot. But they'll be fine now on. Well, they will be once Pedro's arm heals."

"Which reminds me," he said, "I was gonna search for the booze. Lock it away from those two."

"All that's left is a half bottle of brandy," Maddie stated happily, "which is in Daddy O'Hara's office and under lock and key."

Slocum decided to change the subject. "You act like Mace is gonna choose your side if push comes to shove," he said. "Are you forgetting who pays his wages?"

She shook her head, smiling all the while. "I haven't forgotten. But then, you didn't see his face while he was working on those windows. He's a smitten man, Slocum, and if I know how anything operates, it's a smitten man."

Charity giggled. "Oh, just take him to bed, Maddie."

Even Jane's lips curled into a smile, a smile that—for the moment anyway—showed she wasn't thinking about skinning something. She said, "Yes, Maddie. Maybe me and Charity could—"

Slocum brightened, but Maddie pulled him down the hall, saying, "Oh, no, you don't! He's all mine tonight, you cats!"

He heard one of them playfully wail a "meow!" before Maddie closed the bedroom door behind them.

9

Two days later, Slocum found himself worn out, dusty, and waiting at the tiny Vista Verde Livestock Office for somebody named Taggart MacGregor to show up. He'd bought MacGregor's sheep earlier that afternoon from the agent, as arranged by Maddie via telegram. The agent had long since gone home to his supper.

Maddie had crammed the sheep money into his hands that morning, after a night of loving on the bed, on the rug, hanging half out the window, and finally, standing up in the hallway.

"Take the money, you handsome hunk'a love," she'd said, sleepy-eyed and half-teasing. "These were the only merino sheep in the territory, so whatever you do, don't lose them. And get us a good sheep drover or shepherd or whatever they call themselves, and a guard. Get them started on their way, and then you get your backside home as fast as you can."

She'd latched hold of him then, and even after the roughhousing it had taken the night before, his cock had pushed right back at that dainty hand, ready for more.

She hadn't been having any of it, though. "Come back fast, Slocum," she'd repeated in a whisper, and given him a squeeze to remember her by. "And bring this scarred old carcass of a body back with you. With no new scars."

Well, what could a man do?

Ride off into an ambush, it seemed.

A mile out, somebody else—or maybe it was that first somebody—had taken a shot at him, again from far-off cover. This time it had grazed his arm—not hit flesh, but torn a snag in his shirt. There was no cover, so when he'd dived from Bess's back he'd just lain there, playing dead.

When nobody showed up after five minutes, he'd lifted his head just enough to scan the horizon, and he'd seen a little track of blowing dust. It had moved slowly away, as if whoever had drawn down on him was content that he wasn't getting up again.

What made him the maddest—other than the ripped shirt—was that the shooter had just ridden off and left Slocum's horse standing over him out in the middle of nowhere. You'd think he'd at least strip her of her tack and shoo her off to fend for herself!

"G'day, mate," said a curiously accented voice that jarred him from his reverie.

Startled, Slocum looked up and found a skinny, bronze-skinned, blond man leaning in the doorway. There was a shit-eating grin on his face, and what looked like a kid's cap on his head.

"You wouldn't be John Slocum, wouldya?" said the blond fellow in the funny hat.

"Who's askin'?" Slocum asked wearily.

"I'm the fella what's got your sheep," the man replied from the doorway, still grinning. "That is, provided you're Slocum. Always like to ask first. Always like to keep one foot out on the sidewalk till I find out."

Slocum stood up. "You Taggart MacGregor?"

"That'd be me, all right."

"Then I'm Slocum." He stuck his hand out, and the other man took it and gave it a firm shake.

"Glad to make your acquaintance then," said MacGregor. "Wanna see what you bought?"

"You English?" Slocum asked as the two men walked down the dusty street. It was nearly dark, and they passed few people. Slocum was glad for it, if only because nobody could see Taggart MacGregor's hat. He looked like he ought to be wearing knickers and knee socks with it, instead of dusty britches and that fancy snakeskin belt.

"Am I English?" said MacGregor, and then he laughed. "Hell, no. Reckon my people were Scots, way back, like. I'm from Australia. You know, down under? Came over here with a mob of these merinos four years back and took it into my head to stay on. Have a bit of a walkabout Yank-side, y'know?"

Slocum was fairly stumped as to what Mac-

Gregor had just said, but he didn't think it was worth the effort to ask for an explanation.

They came up to the paddock fence then, and both leaned into it, elbows spread wide on the uppermost board.

"Right nice sheep, merinos," MacGregor said. "Dinkum wool, and they can take a fair beatin', weatherwise. Course," he added, adjusting his cap, "Arizona's nothin' compared to the outback. Seen it go up over two hundred degrees at Christmas. Hard-boils eggs between the hen's layin' end and the nest, if you get my drift. These hundred and fifty, they're the last of 'em."

Slocum blinked. Two hundred degrees? And what the hell did dinkum mean? MacGregor was crazier than a loon, all right. But Slocum kept his eyes on the sheep. Crazy or not, MacGregor had the only merinos available in the territory according to Maddie, and Slocum wasn't about to lose them on account of a little thing like insanity.

So he ignored most of what MacGregor had said—babbled was more like it—and said, "The last of which? The chickens or the merinos?" They stank, they were noisy, and if they were anything like all the other sheep he'd met, they were as dumb as a sack of rocks.

"Oh, hell, no!" said MacGregor, straight-faced. "World's crawlin' with 'em. Merinos, I mean, although the world's crawlin' with chickens too. These are just the last of mine. I got the urge to move on again. Five years with you Yanks is enough for me, no offense intended. You ever been to the Sandwich Islands? Hawaii?''

Slocum shook his head slowly.

"Helluva place, helluva place. Or so the books say. Balmy temperatures all year round, volcanoes, sport fishin', no snakes, and women. Lots of women.'' He pushed his little cap back on his head, and there was a dreamy look on his face. ''Got a hanker for some willin' native women, y'know?''

And then Slocum had an idea, and it had nothing to do with island girls. If this bird had lasted five years shooing sheep through cattle land, he was tougher than he looked. He was also bound to last a little longer, crazy or not, although Slocum was beginning to think he was a lot less of a lunatic, and possibly the single biggest exaggerator—not to mention liar—west of the Mississippi.

"Taggart MacGregor, how'd you like to pick up an extra double eagle for two days work, maybe three?'' he asked.

"Twenty dollars?'' MacGregor looked at him with curiosity. "Always eager to feather my nest. What you got in mind?''

"Come with these sheep.''

MacGregor backed off a couple of feet and held up his hands, palms out. Shaking his head, he said, ''No, I've got a bloke lined up for that. Name'a Miguel Farnsworth. He's a Basque—well, half—

and those fellas're wizard with sheep. He'll move your flock and stay on as long as you want—provided you pay him, naturally. But me, I'm going to the salubrious Sandwich Islands.''

Slocum said, ''The agent didn't tell you who was buying your sheep?''

MacGregor dropped his hands. ''Thought *you* were buyin' 'em.''

Slocum shook his head. ''I'm just here with the money. The real buyer is one Maddie O'Hara, up to Three Wives. She's a looker and a half, and she's got two lady partners who are just as good-looking.''

''Yeah, right. And ninety years young too, I'll wager.''

''Oldest isn't a day past twenty-eight, and the youngest is just a touch past twenty.''

MacGregor's lip curled. ''A batch of old maids then. Either too skinny or too fat, or ugly as a batch'a warthdogs.''

''Nope. Flat-out gorgeous, the lot. Left the best whorehouse in Chicago to come out here and ranch sheep. Or farm sheep, or whatever the hell you do with 'em,'' Slocum said.

''Y'know,'' said MacGregor, grinning, ''you may be a big ol' bloke, but I could still flatten you and eat your liver for breakfast.''

''Wouldn't change the fact that there are still three beautiful ladies out in Three Wives, waitin' for their sheep.''

He tried MacGregor's trick, grinning while he added, "Ten-inch waists, three-inch ankles, breasts like over-ripe melons, and bottoms that a man can bury his face and happily suffocate in. A blond, a brunette, and redhead, each with a face that launched a thousand ships. They know all the tricks a century in a harem couldn't teach, and they're rubbin' up against the doorjambs like barn cats in heat, because they ain't none of 'em—with one exception—had a man in a year or better."

MacGregor stared at him for what seemed like a long time, and then he said, "You wouldn't be tryin' to talk 'em down, now would you, Slocum?"

"Somewhat. But stay away from the brunette."

"Yours?"

"As much as she can be anybody's."

MacGregor slowly blew air out through his nose. "Well, mate, me'n Miguel and the dogs'll start the mob out in the morning. Gonna be moving with us, or you in a hurry to get back to that brunette?"

Relieved, Slocum smiled. "I'll see you when you get there." He dug in his pocket, found a piece of paper, and handed it to MacGregor. "That's a map I drew for you. It'll take you the safest route—the easiest for sheep, I think."

MacGregor took it, and shoved it into his pocket. "Ta."

"You carry a gun there, MacGregor? I've been

shot at in the past few days, although I ain't so sure it's got anything to do with sheep. But it's best you know what you're gettin' into.''

MacGregor smiled. "Hell, Miguel's armed to the teeth, what he's got of 'em. And I been making m'livin' off the woollies for a bit of time now. Stands to reason a sheep man always carries a fire-arm or two if he wants to go on bein' a sheep man. And there's always my little Betsy, of course."

"Betsy?"

MacGregor leaned over, reached down, and from his boot scabbard pulled a knife twice as wicked as—and practically twice the size of—an Arkansas toothpick, which was no sissy blade in itself.

Turning the gleaming, serrated, fourteen-inch blade in the last rays of afternoon light, he grinned wide. "Betsy, meet Slocum. Slocum, this here's Betsy."

Slocum smiled and cocked a brow. "Use that little pocket-blade to cut the brim off your hat, did you?"

MacGregor slipped the knife back into its scab-bard. "Y'know, Slocum," he said, "I believe I'm gonna take a likin' to you."

"Fire!" came Pedro's shout. "Fire!"

Maddie opened her eyes to find the room was lit by a horrible orange glow. She leapt out of bed, cracked her shin on the nightstand, and hobbled to the window. The barn was engulfed, and Pedro was trying to toss a bucket of water on it with his one good arm.

"Fire!" he shouted again.

There was no time to waste. She scrambled through the window in her nightgown, ran across the yard in her bare feet, and grabbed the bucket from him.

"Where's Geraldo?" she shouted over the crackle and hiss of the flames, the groans and screams of timber, and the shrill whinnies and frightened squeals and bleats of livestock.

Geraldo appeared at her side in his long underwear, his hair burnt into frizzles. "Here, Señorita."

He pulled the bucket from her hands and tossed it toward the fire, where it hissed and evaporated before it did any good. "The horses and the pigs and the milk cow, they are safe," he shouted before he ran to the trough and filled the bucket again.

It was hopeless. She knew the barn was a lost cause, even as she followed him and filled another pail.

"The house!" she said, pointing. "Wet down the house and the sheds! Get the chickens sopped!"

Jane and Charity were outside by then, and they went to work with a vengeance. Jane cussed up a

storm as she tirelessly cranked the trough pump,
and Charity wept as she passed bucket after bucket
to Maddie and the men, who were wetting down
the outer walls and roof of the house and outbuildings.

At dawn, smeared with soot and soaked in her
own sweat as well as water, Maddie sat on the
porch and surveyed the damage. Fortunately, there
hadn't been any wind to speak of, or the house—
which still stood untouched, except by several
hundred buckets of water—would have gone up
like kindling. The outbuildings were safe, if wet.

The horses, covered in flakes of carbon and
soot, were tethered to a temporary picket line. The
cow and the hogs were staked farther out, looking
forlorn, and the chickens sat inside their little yard
or atop the coop, looking more like dirty and
drowned rats than birds.

There hadn't yet been any time to wonder how
the fire had been started—or more correctly, who
had started it. There'd be plenty of time for re-
criminations and finger-pointing later on.

In the thin light of dawn, Pablo and Geraldo and
Jane still stalked the remnants of the barn, which
was now a pile of black and smoldering rubble.
Pablo and Geraldo worked with rakes and poles,
turning hot timbers and shifting detritus to expose
the fiery pockets. Jane, wearing a pair of Daddy
O'Hara's big boots and a ruined nightgown, followed along with two big buckets, dumping water

on the hot spots. Maddie could hear the water hissing from where she sat.

Charity's head was on her lap, and she was asleep. Sheer exhaustion.

Poor child, Maddie thought dully, as she tried to stroke some of the soot from Charity's strawberry hair. *Poor Jane too. I promised them Eden, and I've given them Hell.*

10

"Damn, Maddie!" Slocum said as they surveyed what was left of the barn. It was two days later, and he'd just ridden in, much to her relief. Trail dust was still thick in the creases of his britches and darkened the furrows in his face, making them appear even deeper.

Maddie took his arm and led him back to the house. She couldn't bear to stand there, looking at the pile of black boards, any longer. It didn't help anything. It just made her sad, and mad too.

"We were thinking," she said as they gained the porch, "that maybe we should just give up. Go back to Chicago."

Slocum started to speak, but she laid two fingers over his lips. If he didn't care that she went back to whoring, or if he didn't care she lost the ranch, even if he was going to argue with her and tell her she was crazy and why didn't she learn to make dresses or keep shop, she didn't want to hear it.

"I said we were thinking about it," she said. "Right after. Charity was even packed up. But we changed our minds. Carl Loomis isn't going to get rid of us that easy."

She leaned her head against his arm. He was so strong, her Slocum: so big and strong and forthright and battle-scarred. He'd never stay, and she'd never ask him, but while he was around, he did lend a girl a great deal of courage.

"He's burned the barn, the sonofabitch," she went on, "and Pedro and Geraldo have rigged temporary corrals for the livestock. If he burns the house, we'll camp out on the ground if we have to, but we're staying."

Slocum shook his head sadly. "Maddie, you're crazier than a yearling filly hip deep in the locoweed. He's already torched your barn. Suppose he kills one of you gals? Or Pedro or Geraldo? He already killed your hired gun. At least, that's what you're convinced of."

She opened the front door. "Then we'll die, won't we? Now, come inside. The girls are getting a bath ready for you."

The girls had filled a bath for him in the tiny back room that existed for that purpose, and Maddie insisted on undressing him.

He fought her on it—he wanted to ride over to Loomis's place and have it out with the bastard right then and there—but she wasn't having it.

"You can kill him tomorrow, Slocum," she said as he eased down into the warm water. "Right now, I'm calling the shots."

The water felt better than he wanted to admit,

and her hands, soaping and massaging his saddle-weary muscles, felt fine. He knew what she had planned for later—her fingers had lingered in certain places quite a bit longer than necessary—so he knew he'd best get the talking out of the way.

"Your sheep'll be here the day after tomorrow, I reckon," he said, resigned to—and, all right, damn glad of—his impending duties as resident stud horse. "Maybe the next. Got your merinos. Bought 'em off an Australian fella named Taggart MacGregor. Both him and the sheep come from clear over on the other side of the world."

"Good," Maddie said, and ran the soapy cloth over his shoulders.

"He's got a man coming with them—a shepherd—that'll stay on."

"Mmm," Maddie said, running the cloth down his spine.

"*He's* coming too," Slocum said. "Gonna stay a while, at least. Looks to be a good man to have around."

"That's nice," she said, and ran the washcloth around his side.

"Promised him twenty dollars and all the naked and willin' women he wanted."

The washcloth stopped.

"Except the brunette."

The washcloth moved again. "He'll have to take that up with Jane and Charity."

"Reckon he can do that, probably with both of

'em at once.'' He smiled. ''He's a powerful talker.''

The washcloth traveled down his belly, and he knew where it was headed. He also knew he'd better talk fast.

''You know for certain it was Loomis that started the fire?''

The washcloth stopped again. ''Who else?''

''I mean, it couldn't have been a lantern somebody forgot, or a careless match?''

She sat back, bringing the washcloth with her—much to Slocum's chagrin. ''It was almost four in the morning. Everybody'd been asleep for hours.''

''Who was on watch?''

''Pedro. He's the one that started the alarm.'' Her brow furrowed. ''Say, you aren't insinuating that Pedro—''

He fastened a wet hand on her shoulder. ''I'm not insinuating a damn thing, Maddie. I'm just tryin' to get all the facts.''

She frowned. ''Loomis sent somebody over here to start that fire. That's a fact.''

The mention of Loomis sending someone reminded him, and he asked, ''Maddie, is Mace still showing up to work on the house?''

''And to sing, drat it, although he'd already been and gone for hours by the time the fire started,'' she said. ''And don't think I didn't consider him.''

He grinned. "You gals didn't do anything rash to ol' Mace, now did you?"

She hesitated.

"Maddie?"

"Well, Jane sort of shot him."

Slocum rubbed his hand over his face. "Shit, Maddie! Why didn't you tell me! And why'd you let Jane—"

"Oh, pish!" she said, sitting up straight. "She only shot his hat off, Slocum!"

He was about to comment on the rank propensity for hat-shooting in these parts, but she didn't take a breath.

"Besides, he quit Loomis," she said. "I hired him, and his little brother too. They'll be bunking in the toolshed, for your information. And if you're wondering why you didn't see them when you rode in, I sent them to town to pick up grain and hay and straw, and to see if we couldn't get a little more credit from the mercantile."

She must have read the expression his face then, because she added quickly, "And they're not a couple of mooncalves. A little lovesick maybe, but they do their work."

He took her hand and placed it—and the washrag—on his chest. "And how you plannin' to pay them?"

She started rubbing his chest—a little too hard—and said, "I'll think of a way."

"Anything else happen that you want to tell me

about?'' he said. ''A legion of Russian cavalry turn up on the south forty? Did it rain frogs? One'a the mares give birth to a three-headed dragon?''

Her hand stopped again, then gave his chest a swat. ''Other than the barn burning and the new hands and the eviction notice from the bank, not a goddamned thing.''

Slocum closed his eyes. Women could be the damnedest things! He opened them again and said, ''Maddie? Honey? What notice from the bank?''

''Well, it was from Whit Cramer anyway. And I got it before you left.''

''What?''

''Whit's the only lawyer Three Wives has got,'' she continued, as if he hadn't spoken, ''and he's also the president of the bank. Maybe it wasn't from the bank,'' she said thoughtfully, then frowned. ''Maybe he just used their stationery, the cheap so-and-so.''

''And this notice said?'' Slocum urged.

''That we've been using Carl Loomis's water for twenty years, and now he wants either his water back or a whole lot of money. You know, if you keep on talking, this water's going to get cold.''

She fished around for the soap. ''There's no sense in talking about Loomis's stupid suit, because I'm not going to pay. I'm going to ignore it. He can foreclose all he wants, but it won't do any good.''

"Maddie—"

"Possession is nine-tenths of the law."

If there was one thing Slocum had learned in all his years, it was that when you're sitting stark-naked in a tub of soapy water, and the lady with the washrag has just told you in so many words to either shut up or put your pants back on, you shut up.

"Yes, ma'am," he said teasingly, and slid this new information to the back of his brain. For now. "Whatever you say, ma'am. You suppose you could get back to washin' this old cowboy? I was just beginning to admire the direction it was takin'."

Maddie let the air out of her cheeks with a hiss and shook her head. "You beat everything, you know that?"

"Been told," he said, closing his eyes. The cloth started to move downward again.

"And where the Sam Hill did you find an extra twenty dollars for this Taggart MacGregor fellow?" she said so suddenly that it took him a minute to remember who Taggart MacGregor was.

"I gave you everything we had, Slocum," she went on. "It was the last of our money."

"Reckon I can find it someplace."

"Reckon you'd better. We're already rubbing shoulders with the poorhouse, what with two Cantrell boys on the payroll."

She had hold of his cock by then, had hold of

it by that warm, slippery washcloth, and began to move the rag slowly up and down the length of it.

"Nice," he said, his eyes still closed. "I'll give you about ten minutes to stop that."

"Oh," said Maddie's voice, close to his ear, "you'll give me a lot longer than that, Slocum."

And then she was in the tub with him, stark naked, although he had no idea how she'd gotten that way. Her knees were caught, on either side of his hips, against the narrow iron walls of the tub. Her fanny rested against his bent knees, and her breasts, wet and glistening with droplets, rode just above the waterline and pushed against his chest.

Slocum knew what to do. He kissed her, long and hard, and then pushed her back at the same time he freed first one of her knees, then the other. Slowly, her knees rose toward his armpits while her fanny sank into the water, lower, lower, until, sighing with delight, she was impaled on his shaft.

"God, Slocum," she breathed, leaning back against his wet thighs, her eyes half-lidded. "You sure do know how to fill a gal up."

He said nothing, just lifted his arms, took a breast in each hand, and began running his thumbs over the nipples. They were pink and puckered, and slippery with soap.

Maddie closed her eyes the rest of the way. "I do believe," she murmured, "that if you stayed as big as you are inside me, and kept up with that rubbing, I could come all by myself."

"Fat chance," he whispered, and gave his hips a little buck. It was a difficult feat in the narrow tub, but Maddie's gasp made it worthwhile. "Get to work, gal."

She did, but not in the usual sense. She leaned forward, kissing him, and then she began to slowly gyrate her hips while she pulled at him with secret internal muscles. Her fanny never moved up or down, but began a sinuous dance over him, around him: figure-eighting, then circling. And all the while those muscles kept clenching and unclenching, squeezing, rippling.

"Jesus, Maddie!" he gasped. "Where'd you learn to do that?"

And then he couldn't talk anymore. He could only feel her body—her breasts, her lips, her torso, her arms—slithering against him in the water, feel her insides squeezing and kneading his cock in a way so peculiar and foreign it was as if he'd never had a woman before. He felt her leading him, toying with him, playing him like a harp—first she plucked one string, then another, and he never knew where it was going, only that it was the most beautiful music he could imagine.

He surrendered to her ministrations, letting his arms go limp, his eyelids droop, feeling all of his sensations center in his cock, which seemed to be growing larger still, impossibly huge. He pushed his head back against the tall backrest of the tub, and still she kept moving, unrelentingly squeezing and releasing with those smooth, slick muscles, rotating her hips slowly over him, jailing him whole in a prison of velvet, driving him mad.

And then he came in an enormous explosion, all fire and fury, and he couldn't help but buck his hips up into her. It was only when he was regaining some sense of where he was and who he was that he realized she'd been overcome too and was shuddering against him, whispering his name.

He put his arms around her and hugged her to him. He stroked her hair. It was as black as obsidian, as glossy as a raven's wing shining blue-black in the morning sun.

"Maddie," he whispered as he kissed the top of her head. He was still inside her, and he could feel her belly thrumming with the aftershocks of what they'd just done.

"Darlin' Maddie girl. Every time I think I have you figured, you come up with something new."

She lifted her face toward him. Drowsy-eyed and half-smiling, she murmured, "Shut up and kiss me, Slocum."

11

Jane had been testy with him all afternoon, but when supper came round and they were all gathered at the table, she slammed the plate down in front of Slocum with enough force to slop gravy over the table cloth.

"Jane!" said Maddie, leaping up.

"It's all right, honey," said Slocum, waving a hand as Maddie sopped the gravy up with a rag.

He watched as Jane walked away without a word. A strange bird, that one, and mightily riled about something. She'd been riled since he rode in, that first day. But now she was taking it to new heights. He wasn't quite sure if she was het up about anything specific, though, or if it was just his presence that was ticking her off.

"Jane?" he called.

"Biscuits in a minute," she replied, her back to him as she stood over the stove.

"I want to talk to you."

She turned, glaring at him. The others at the table—Charity, Mace and Mike Cantrell, Pedro, Geraldo, and Maddie—all froze over their plates. She had them trained, he'd say that for her.

He shoved back his chair, set his napkin on the table, and gestured toward the door. "Outside, if you wouldn't mind."

She held her ground. "And if I would?"

"I can always carry you out."

She seemed to consider it, then at last she gave a sniff and went out to the porch. Slocum followed her into the evening, and shut the door behind them.

Immediately, she folded her arms. "What?" she said accusingly.

He wasn't in the mood to shilly-shally. He said, "Who stuck the bee up your butt, Jane? Ever since I rode in here you've been as testy as a land-locked snappin' turtle, or else horny to beat the band. Maybe you're just being so all-fired cussed because I saw you naked and teasing Mace right off the bat. I don't know what else it could be, but I don't rightly care enough to find out."

She opened her mouth, doubtless to spit venom in his direction, but he held up a hand and went on.

"The only thing I know for sure—the only thing that's important right now—is that you gals are in a world of trouble out here. Your hired gun got himself killed—and why or by whom isn't the big question right at the moment.

"When I rode in, I reckon that gave you gals some hope. But the day I ride out to go buy those damn sheep for Maddie, somebody leaves me for dead on the desert. And somebody delivers an eviction notice, and somebody else burns down the barn.''

Jane's lips twisted, but she didn't speak. Judging from her expression, though, he was glad she didn't have a gun handy.

"Seems to me that somebody had to tell Loomis—assuming that he's the bad apple in all this—that I was gone. Maybe somebody told him I wasn't coming back, and that he could finally scare Maddie off for good and all. I been thinkin' that maybe—just maybe—that somebody was you.''

"Drop dead, Slocum,'' she said at last. "How do you even know if I know how to use a gun?''

"You're pretty good with it around Mace,'' he said. "You miss when you want to and hit him when you want to. Hell, Jane, I don't know beans about where you come from. You could be from a whole family of sharpshooters, for all I know.''

"You can take your stupid accusations and stuff 'em where the sun don't shine. Or maybe,'' she added, a dangerous smile curving over her lips, "you'd like me to do it for you.''

"What I'd like is for you to come clean, Jane,'' he said, trying his best to ignore her tone. "I've got enough problems without you playin' games. I'm not Mace. I don't fool so easy.''

She sneered. "All of you are just nasty little boys. What is it you want, Slocum? A free ride?

Want a little show? Want to take on me and Charity too? Isn't Maddie enough for you, big man?''

Suddenly, she hiked up her skirts, lifting them to her waist. "This what you want, big man?''

Slocum slapped her across the face before he realized what he was doing.

She dropped the skirts, but she didn't flinch. All she did was slowly raise a hand to her cheek, and as she did, she smiled. It was like looking into the eyes of a snake, and despite himself and the weather, Slocum felt a chill.

"I see," she said. "That's how it is."

"Sorry," he offered, although he didn't half-mean it. "Didn't intend to hit you."

"Yes, you did," she said, still smiling coldly. "You all do."

And then, without another word, she turned on her heel and went back inside.

It was two in the morning, and cool. And with the exception of Geraldo, who was standing guard up on the ridge, Slocum was the only soul awake.

Despite the chill, he sat on the porch in just his britches and his gun belt, and he was smoking one of the late Daddy O'Hara's Havanas. Fine cigars, and only half a dozen of them left. He knew he should be doling them out, stretching them out to last longer, but he had a gnarly problem—one that needed a measure of good, mellow, Cuban tobacco smoke to help sort it out.

Bess, along with Maddie's horses, was out in the corral. Three sides of it had already been standing, more or less. The fourth, which had previously been made up by the south side of the barn, which was now burned to the ground, was temporarily closed by thrown-together stacks of burnt timbers, bales of hay and straw hauled from town by Mace and Mike, a buckboard, and a Sunday-go-to-meeting buggy.

Farther out, he could just make out the outline of the stacks of adobe bricks Pablo and Geraldo—and more recently, Mace and Mike—had been making, ready to bake in tomorrow's sun.

Timber was at a premium out here. Adobe was the smart construction material. Besides, he thought, rolling his ash off on the wooden arm of his chair, it didn't burn worth a damn.

His thoughts were all over the place. It seemed as if every time he got half a handle on what the hell was going on, something else happened that blew down his logic like a house of cards in a cyclone. Either that, or Maddie came sniffing after him.

He smiled. He didn't mind Maddie's attentions, not one bit.

But still, he tried one more time to organize his thoughts.

He'd found a dead man in the desert, probably Taylor by name, possibly killed by Loomis's men. Or not.

He decided to put that one aside for the time being. There was enough confusion without it, and closer to home.

All right. In one camp, he had Mr. Carl Loomis, head of the local Cattlemen's Association. Of course, it didn't look like Mr. Loomis had a single steer, but then, it was autumn. They might be in the high country.

This Mr. Loomis was opposed to the ladies, because the ladies were bringing in sheep. Also because he seemed to have the lamebrained notion that if he kicked them off their land, they'd file straight into his ready-made whorehouse and settle down to work without so much as a peep of protest, instead of hopping the nearest stage and waving him good-bye and good riddance.

That last one—Loomis's whorehouse—still didn't make a lick of sense, but Slocum decided to go past it for the moment.

The method by which Loomis was trying to get the ladies off Maddie's land was puzzling, for certain. He'd riled up his men—or maybe he hadn't, if Mace was to be believed—and sent them over to shoot the place up. He seemed to have the town banker—who was also the town lawyer—in his back pocket, and he'd taken legal action, suing Maddie for water theft, retroactive for two decades. Two decades!

In addition to this, he'd sent somebody over to burn them out.

Now why, Slocum wondered, would a man with the gall to sue for water—and the sand to think there was any way in hell to coerce these gals to work for him—be so stupid as to start a fire, especially right on the heels of serving the legal papers?

Furthermore, Slocum had been thinking about those water rights. Maddie got most of her water from a well, and that well had not only supplied enough water to dampen a barn fire, but also to give him a bath and water all the livestock, and still it had showed no signs of being taxed.

Out of curiosity, he'd checked the well—not the livestock pump or the hand pump in the house, but the old well, the original one, in the pump house. He'd lowered a lantern deep into it, and found that the mineral ring was still sitting right at the waterline. All that water used up, and it hadn't gone down so much as an inch.

Furthermore, it seemed to be flowing. He'd brought along some dinner scraps, and dropped a couple of slices of cake down there. They'd hung for a few seconds, dropping slowly in the water, and then something had tugged then down and away.

Current.

He made a mental note to ask Maddie if she had any maps of the place.

And people kept shooting at him. No, he corrected himself, not people. One person. He—or she—had to be a pretty fair marksman too. After all, both times he'd gotten a piece of Slocum, even though it was just sartorial.

He wished now that he hadn't accused Jane. At least, not until he had collected more intelligence on the matter. It wasn't like him to go off half-cocked. But by thunder, she annoyed the piss out of him! Poor old Mace had sure picked the wrong lady to be smitten with, that was all he had to say.

At least Mace'd had the sense to hold off on the serenade tonight. Slocum had a feeling that if Jane had heard so much as one wobbly note outside her window, she would have just blown his fool head off instead of his hat.

That goddamn Jane!

He took another angry puff on the cigar, and forced himself to stop being annoyed at Jane and concentrate on the matter at hand.

The townspeople. They were scared, all right, but what was it they were afraid of? Carl Loomis? Maddie? Maybe they were afraid of sheep. He'd seen people in cow country react all out of character at the merest mention of sheep. But still . . .

At a small sound behind him, he turned, drawing his gun out of habit. But it was only Maddie, wrapped in his shirt and nothing else. On her, it seemed huge.

"Want company?" she asked softly, putting her small, white hand on his shoulder. It looked like a bird sitting there, he thought, a white dove perched on a weatherbeaten old fence post.

"In bed," he said, rising to the accompaniment of his creaking bones. He put his arm around her. "Let's go in, but to sleep, all right? I'm gonna ride out tomorrow morning and meet Taggart MacGregor."

12

Slocum had been riding three hours when he finally spotted the approaching trail dust of the flock. Urging Bess into a lope, he soon spied the first of the sheep coming over a small desert rise, then the rest, then the three dogs hot on their heels. There was no sign of Taggart MacGregor for a few moments, but then he appeared at the crest. He was on foot, and pulling a travois.

Slocum let the sheep go on by, then rode up to him.

"What the hell are you doing on foot, MacGregor?" was the first thing that came out of his mouth. "Where's your horse?"

"Never use 'em," the Aussie said with a grin. "Though I'll admit that fancy brumby of yours is gonna come in right handy, what with Miguel stove up."

For the first time, Slocum noticed the occupant of the travois. He was dark—a Basque, MacGregor had said—and more colorfully dressed than Slocum would have expected of an old man, for he looked to be near seventy. His pants were dark green, with a yellow sash holding up his britches. A violet shirt, and a cap, black trimmed with red rickrack, topped it. He was also wounded in the hip.

He parted his lips and smiled, showing a gold eyetooth and a black gap where his two front teeth should have been, but he said nothing.

"Miguel don't say much," MacGregor explained. He whistled at the dogs in a complicated series of patterns, although he made them seem effortless.

Two dogs immediately ran out in front of the flock, spaced wide. They dropped to the ground, eyeing the sheep, who stopped as if stricken. The third dog went out to the right, then dropped.

"Fact is, he doesn't talk at all. Fell in with the wrong sort of cowboys a few years back," MacGregor continued, as if these whistle-trained dogs were a common, everyday sort of thing. "Seems they took exception to his tongue and cut it out. Isn't that right, Miguel?"

Miguel nodded.

Slocum blinked. He had no idea what to say.

"Course," MacGregor went on as he opened his canteen and lifted it to his lips, "they were bad at it. Only took half, so Miguel can still whistle with the best of 'em."

As if to prove this, Miguel suddenly whistled. To Slocum, it sounded like a sort of crazy birdcall, but one of the lead dogs jumped to its feet, circled the flock at a flying trot, and came back to sit beside the travois.

Miguel whistled again, soft and low, and the dog put his head in his lap and gazed up adoringly.

"By Jesus, I needed that," said MacGregor, wiping his mouth on his sleeve. He offered the canteen to Miguel, who waved it away. Recapping it, he squinted up at the sun, then turned to Slocum. "Much farther, is it?"

Slocum shook his head. "Who the hell shot him?" he asked, although he was fairly certain he knew the answer. Generally, at least.

But MacGregor said, "Oh, no worries there, mate. The old pelican was just showin' me how this sheila used to dance on a tabletop at this place outside Swelter Falls, and he fell off the rock he was dancin' on. Landed on his knife." He looked over at Miguel. "See? I told you, you shouldn't go drinkin' and dancin'."

Miguel raised his hands and shrugged his shoulders, and the dog climbed into the travois between his feet, turned three times, and lay down.

Slocum sighed. As usual, he only understood about a third of the babble that came out of MacGregor's mouth, and even then, it tended to be exaggerations or downright lies.

Still, you couldn't help but like the cuss. He was just too damned good-natured to hate.

Slocum spanked Bess on the rump, moving her over. "Let's get her hitched to the travois then.

Better get moving if we want to make Maddie's by nightfall.''

They were about a mile and a quarter from the ranch when the hair on the back of Slocum's neck began to bristle.

A minute later, he saw the first man.

He was about a two hundred yards out, and sat his mount atop a red rock bluff, silhouetted against the late afternoon sky. There was a rifle in his hand.

A scan of the horizon brought two more men— mounted as well—into view. Then another.

"Got company," said MacGregor, walking beside him as he led Bess, with the travois and its passenger.

MacGregor's pace never varied. "You reckon these are some'a Loomis's blokes?"

"Reckon," said Slocum. He was trying to figure the best place to send the sheep, because it looked to him as if there was going to be a gun battle, and he didn't suppose Maddie would be too happy about having spent the tail end of her cash for a dead flock.

"Aw, don't look so worried, mate," MacGregor said. "There's only four of 'em." He looked to the right. "No, five."

"Great," said Slocum. Neither man had given any noticeable sign that he'd seen the riders as yet. "Any ideas?"

"Well," said MacGregor, not altering his stride, "I'm gonna whistle these dogs to take the woollies straight through, just as fast as their little hooves can carry 'em, and while they're doin' that, I figured we could jump into that patch of brush up ahead and start shooting."

"Nice idea," replied Slocum. "Except that we've got a rider coming in."

He stopped then, half-glad for the break, even if it meant he'd get shot. His muscles were accustomed to riding, not trudging through the desert, and his calves and feet burned from all the walking. MacGregor and Miguel might be used to all this tramping around, but it was about to do Slocum in. Not that he'd let on to MacGregor, of course.

The rider, portly and a little red-faced, walked his horse up easy, cutting through the flock. He held a bandanna over his nose, and kept it there until he was about fifteen feet from them. Then he lowered it and, sour-faced, said, "Christ, but these critters got a stench!"

MacGregor smiled and said, "Why, that's Aussie perfume, mate!"

The horseman, who Slocum assumed to be Loomis by his age and carriage—and by his belly—ignored MacGregor entirely and addressed Slocum. "You the man who's took up with those whores?"

"If you mean the man who's staying at Maddie

O'Hara's place,'' he said, ''then yes, guess I am. You Loomis?''

''That'd be me,'' the horseman said with no small degree of vanity. Slocum took him for a man who was more than a little sold on his own importance. Smugly, he added, ''Guess you heard of me.''

Slocum nodded. ''You'd guess right.''

''And you'd be Slocum?''

He nodded. ''That I would.'' The dogs were moving the sheep farther and farther away, but MacGregor didn't seem to care, or even to notice.

Well, if the sheepman wasn't worried, Slocum supposed he shouldn't be either. He pushed back his concern—about the sheep anyway—and said to Loomis, ''If you boys rode all the way out here to say howdy and welcome to the neighborhood, I'm beholden' to you. Right neighborly. In fact, you can help us move these sheep, if you're of a mind.''

''Well, now, Slocum,'' Loomis said, leaning forward, his forearm on the saddlehorn, ''you read my mind.''

Slocum didn't like the look of his smile. He also didn't care for the fact that the others were riding closer, coming in.

Loomis continued. ''See, we thought we'd help you turn 'em.''

''Turn 'em into what?'' MacGregor piped up, like an idiot. ''Coyote food?''

Loomis stopped smiling. "As a matter of fact, yes."

He reached a hand to his gun, and then all hell broke loose.

MacGregor leapt for Loomis's gun hand and yanked him off his horse, at the same time letting out a series of sharp whistles.

Before Slocum could draw his gun or figure who to aim it at—even before Loomis hit the ground—Miguel's lapdog went flying past and the two others rocketed away from the flock, and they were attacking the other riders' horses. Snarling, they leapt at the horses' hind quarters, barking with a frenzy, tearing the riders' heels, then snaking in to bite low on the horses' pasterns.

The horses were bucking and hopping and kicking, the dogs darting from the path of pistoning hooves, finding new targets with startling precision, striking, then dodging away. And suddenly, what had started out as a very tense situation—to say the least—turned into a free-for-all.

One cowboy lost his reins. The last Slocum saw of him, he was hanging on for dear life while his mount crow-hopped and sunfished his way toward the distant horizon.

Another—Slocum thought it was Ed Barlow—went sailing, and moment he landed there was a dog standing on his chest, growling into his face, daring him to twitch a muscle.

The other two were still nearby, still on their

crazed horses, still clinging to their saddlehorns. Well, barely.

MacGregor, whose knife was against Loomis's throat, said, "Enough, mate?"

Loomis swallowed, then nodded.

MacGregor grinned over at Slocum. "Well, 'tweren't really fair. Next time he'll know t'bring a bigger mob." With a wink, he pulled Loomis up, then pushed him away. Loomis stumbled again, and landed with a soft *squish* at Slocum's feet.

MacGregor, whistling orders at the dogs, calmly walked off to collect the others.

Loomis rose to his knees. "Shit!" he cursed, picking up his hat. "Shit!"

Slocum, his gun drawn, saw Loomis rise up, and saw what he was rising up from—a pile of fresh sheep droppings.

"Tsk, tsk," Slocum clucked. "Looks like that sheep stench you were complainin' about is gonna follow you home."

Loomis's red face went even redder. Still on one knee, he muttered through clenched teeth, "Screw you, Slocum."

"Funny you should bring that up, Mr. Loomis," Slocum said, thumbing back his hat. "That's another thing I been wanting to talk to you about. Screwin', that is."

Loomis gained his feet at last. Far behind him, Slocum saw Wally rounding up the last of Loomis's

hands. The dogs, who seemingly never got a rest—
nor needed one, by the looks of them—were already far away and bunching up the last of the scattered and bawling sheep. The dog who'd held Ed
Barlow at bay, a bobtailed blue merle, was faced off
with a recalcitrant ram.

Despite himself, Slocum grinned. That sheep
didn't know it, but he didn't have a chance.

"I've heard of you," Loomis growled, and Slocum force his attention back to business.

"You already said that."

With his hat, Loomis swatted at the sheep dung
still clinging to his pants, and only succeeded in
soiling the brim. He looked up angrily. "You were
hooked up with that Reb scum, Cole Younger,
weren't you?"

"Ancient history," Slocum replied.

"And you rode with Toothy Jack Morrison up
on the Rim."

"I'm here now," Slocum said, and what little
patience he had left was slowly sipping away.
"Why are you so dead set on runnin' these gals
off their land, Loomis?"

Loomis scowled. "You ought to know. You're
pushin' the reason."

He tipped his head back toward the flock, now
in a tight group and standing still. The dogs were
all lying down, forming a triangle around the flock
about fifteen feet out, seemingly controlling the
sheep by the simple force of their will.

Slocum shook his head. "No, I don't think so. You ought to know, Loomis, that this is lousy land for cattle. As a matter of fact, I think you *do* know it. I haven't seen one single, solitary steer out here. Not even a maverick."

Loomis frowned and pursed his lips.

"Now," Slocum continued, "I could be wrong, but I suspect you've got your herd up in the high country, and you're keeping them there year-round. I don't believe these little sheep of Maddie's are what's caught in your craw."

"Sheep ruin the land," Loomis spat. "Everybody knows that."

"Oh, horseshit," Slocum barked. "Besides the fact that this land is worthless for grazin' cows, you and I both know that sheep and cattle can graze side by side. Least, that's what the college boys are sayin'. Myself, I've seen 'em grazed on the same pastures for years with no harm come to it. It don't make me like sheep any more than I did—I'm averse to 'em on general principle—but it shoots the hell out of that old wives' tale, so stop mouthing it."

Loomis glared at him.

"So I reckon," Slocum went on, "that these woollies are just an excuse you're using to move Maddie O'Hara off her land. Those gals don't scare easy, Loomis, in case you hadn't noticed."

Slocum rubbed at his forehead thoughtfully. It

was time for the big question. At least, it was big to him.

"I been wonderin'," he said, "just how you plan to move those gals into your fancy ginger-breaded whorehouse, Loomis. Just what in the name of U.S. Grant makes you think that even if you did pry 'em off that ranch, they'd come merrily skippin' on down to the town brothel, liftin' their knickers?"

Loomis looked at him as if he were simple. "Why, the water, of course!"

"What?" Maddie'd mentioned something about water rights, but he guessed it had slipped his mind in all the excitement. He must be getting old.

"They owe me," Loomis said. He tried wiping at his soiled hat with his bandanna, to no avail. "They owe me a debt that their lousy, played-out ranch can't satisfy. I have the law on my side!"

"I doubt that."

"You just wait!" Loomis railed. "Come the first, Sheriff Ward Semple will be out there, moving them to town at gunpoint, if need be. I'll have these sheep shot and left for the coyotes, those traitors Mace and Mike Cantrell run out of the territory on a rail, and Miss Fancy-Britches Maddie O'Hara workin' flat on her back for the next fifteen years."

And then, suddenly, he smiled. "I'm a fair man, though, Slocum. Five years each, if her lady friends decide to stick around and help her out.

Loyalty can be a real fine thing. I admire that in a person, and I'm willin' to make allowances.''

"You know, Loomis," Slocum growled, "you're awful goddamned smart-alecky for somebody who's standing on the wrong end of a cocked Colt.''

Fortunately for Loomis, that was the moment MacGregor chose to march his three remaining hapless cowhands within spitting distance.

Ed Barlow, who'd been thrown, was limping badly. The other two hands, who Slocum recognized from the hoorah at the ranch that first day, weren't moving along any too sprightly, either.

He supposed any of these boys could bust broncs all day and, for the most part, come out none the worse for wear. They looked to be a tough bunch, even if they didn't appear to be the smartest crew that ever came down the pike.

But having your horse suddenly attacked by a ball of fur and fangs that didn't give up—especially when you were all set for some good old rowdy-dow that only included gunplay and maybe some target practice with sheep as the targets— was the sort of thing that took a fellow by short hairs when he was least expecting it. And yanked hard.

Yanked him right off his horse, in one case.

MacGregor smiled. "Got their guns. What you want to do with 'em? Personally, I was thinkin' about strippin' them to the skin and stakin' them out someplace real sunny. But then I remembered that I done that only last week. Wouldn't want to repeat myself so soon.''

Slocum considered the situation. Then he picked up Loomis's horse's reins and stepped up on the big bay.

Before Loomis could shout, "Horse thief!" Slocum said, "Let's be neighborly about it, Mac-Gregor, and all walk back together. Well, you'll walk. You don't mind walkin', do you, Loomis?''

A grinning MacGregor clapped Loomis on the shoulder. "No worries, mate. Exercise'll do wonders for that belly!''

13

So Loomis was holding Maddie liable for the use of the water he claimed was his—and this was how he planned to populate the Three Wives bordello?

Riding high on the cattleman's big bay alongside the bleating flock, Slocum shook his head at the sheer bark of it. Loomis had balls, he'd give him that—maybe not too much in the way of logic, but balls he most certainly had.

He had a feeling that one look at a survey map would put that claim to rest. He figured Maddie's water was coming from an underground spring or river, entirely separate from the Blue Calf, the stream that Loomis was claiming for his own. If Slocum was correct, a map would show him where Maddie's river came to the surface.

He had a gut feeling that Loomis was hiding something, something big. Getting Maddie and her friends off that land by hook or by crook was just the first step.

Up ahead, in the middle of the flock, Loomis and his boys tripped along, hobbling and hopping on feet unaccustomed to making progress in anything other than a leather stirrup. That old ram had taken exception to Loomis's britches for some reason—you'd think he would have accepted them, what with the manure stains, but there you were—and every once in a while he butted Loomis from the rear.

It was dangerous business, considering the ram's big, curved horns. But Slocum, safe on horseback, was willing to take the chance.

He led the rest of the Loomis boys' mounts, and behind him, behind the flock, MacGregor led Bess and the travois that bore Miguel. MacGregor didn't even look winded, let alone sore. He was smiling, joking with Miguel.

Slocum thought again of the recent confrontation with Loomis's men. It could have gone bad, very bad, if MacGregor hadn't thought quickly, and if he hadn't had a secret arsenal in those crazy mutts of his. Slocum reached in his pocket and brought out his fixings. Those damned dogs beat everything.

As he rolled himself a quirlie, he remembered the fine Havanas waiting back at the ranch. And the fine woman. Just a day had gone by, and he was hungry for her again. Hell, even after twenty minutes without her, he was hungry for her.

That Maddie. She lit fires in places he didn't even know he had kindling!

He struck a lucifer and lit up just about the time that Loomis, who was just recovering from another ram-induced stumble, turned around and shook a pudgy fist at him.

"How much goddamned longer, Slocum?" he shouted back, scattering the sheep in his vicinity. "My men and me need a rest!"

"You'll get your rest soon enough," Slocum called up to him. His smoke in hand, he pointed ahead, toward the horizon. "Ranch ought to be nudgin' up any time now."

Even as he said the words, the peak of the roof appeared in the distance.

Home.

And Maddie.

He left Loomis and his men in the care of MacGregor and Miguel, and loped ahead, to the house.

Geraldo, who was just heading from the make-shift adobe brickworks to the house, swerved and walked out to meet him.

"*Señor*? Slocum! *Hola!*" he called. "We have just seen the dust of your herd. Well," he added philosophically, "maybe it is not a herd. What do you call a herd of sheep?"

"Trouble," muttered Slocum, dismounting.

"Very good, Slocum!" Geraldo said, laughing. "I like that. 'A trouble of sheep.' " He took Slocum's reins and, frowning, looked the bay up and down. "Something happen to the black Appaloosa mare you ride, Señor? She was *muy bonita*. This bay is jug-headed, if you do not mind my saying."

"No," Slocum said, and waved at the crowd making bricks, gesturing them over. "Don't mind a bit. And my mare's busy haulin' a cut-up Basque sheep man with no tongue."

"*Que?*"

"Never mind."

As the group from the brickworks neared, wiping adobe from their hands and flipping the tan mud from their skirts or trousers, Slocum frowned. "Geraldo, I see everybody but Maddie. She up to the house?"

Geraldo shook his head. "No, she say she has something important to do. She rides off, oh, about eleven. Before lunch anyway."

Slocum gritted his teeth. It was already close to sunset. "And you let her? With people gettin' shot at and the sheep comin' in and the threats that've been made, you let her ride out on her own?"

Geraldo shrugged. "She is the boss. Is not my job to tell her what to do."

"It's your job to show some sense," he grumbled. "Shit. Well, which way'd she go?"

Geraldo pointed.

Damn it anyway. Now, instead of putting everybody together and figuring out this idiot thing, he was going to have to go find Maddie, if she hadn't gotten her fool head shot off or fallen down a ravine or tried to chuck a cougar under the chin.

"Mace!" he shouted to the motley group, which was just wandering over to where he and Geraldo stood. "Saddle me that blue roan gelding out of the corral, and hurry up about it."

Mace turned on his heel and trotted back toward the makeshift corral without question.

"Got us a mess of adobe blocks piled up," Mike said happily as he caught up with the rest of the workers. His voice only cracked once. "Geraldo here says by tomorrow we'll have enough to start buildin' a new barn."

"Not building, Miguelito," Geraldo said, shaking his head. "Not until they cure. But we have very many. Soon, we will need more straw."

"Aw, stop callin' me that Mexican name, Geraldo," Mike protested, but he laughed when Geraldo pushed his hat back and ruffled his blond hair.

"Slocum? What is it?" Charity asked. Her strawberry hair was stuffed up under a floppy old hat, and there were adobe smudges on her cheeks and nose. Somehow, she managed to make it look pretty.

Jane, on the other hand, didn't look at him. She stared out toward the sheep. He could hear their bawls now, just faintly. "Who's that walking along with them?" Jane asked, still rubbing at the adobe staining her wrists. There was no hint of a smile in her voice.

"Your friend, Carl Loomis, and a few of his stalwart employees," Slocum said. "They sorta rode out to say howdy."

Jane spat on the ground.

Slocum ignored her. He said, "There's two fellas with those sheep that belong with 'em: Taggart MacGregor—he's got a foreign accent and he's kind of funny in the head, but he's a good man in a pinch—and a fella named Miguel who's gonna need some medical attention. Fell on his knife. As for the rest of 'em, you can send 'em packing. Hand over their horses but not their guns— MacGregor has got them—and shoo 'em on their way."

Mace came up then, leading the blue roan at a trot, and Slocum swung a leg up over the horse before it was fully stopped.

"Don't talk to 'em, don't argue with 'em, don't say a word," he continued. "And Taggart MacGregor is in charge till I get back. Understand?"

Pablo and Geraldo nodded, as did the Cantrell boys and Charity. Jane just scowled at him, but he supposed, for her, it was as close to a "yes" as he was going to get.

He reined the horse around, kicked it in the flanks, and set off toward the southeast, toward Maddie, at a gallop.

14

He rode up on Maddie an hour later. The sun was about halfway set—and his stomach had set into growling—and he was just wondering if there'd be enough moon tonight to track by, when she rode right over the cactus-covered crest of the small hill and smack into him.

"Shit!" was the first thing he said to her. "What if I'd been one of Loomis's boys?"

She reined her horse up next to his. "Hello yourself. And, I might ask, what if *I'd* been one of Loomis's men? Seems to me your goose would have been cooked too."

He didn't care to answer that. Dang her for asking all the wrong questions anyhow! And just when he had a goodly head of steam built up about her taking off on her own!

So he just said, "Your sheep are here, safe and sound."

"That's wonderful, Slocum!" She reined around him and started back toward the ranch house. "Please tell me they're really merinos?"

He followed suit, riding alongside her. "A sheep is a sheep to me. But the fella I bought 'em from said that's what they were."

"Wonderful! I could just kiss you!"

"They threw in a shepherd and three dogs, and like I told you, the previous owner came along for the ride. You got any maps back at the house?"

She smiled. "You're so romantic, Slocum."

"Cut me some slack, Maddie," he said, too tired to grin. "Most of the time you keep my brain so occupied that I don't have time to notice half the hijinks going on around me."

"Thank you," she said, still smiling slyly. "And I believe Daddy O'Hara kept a few maps, yes. A room full of them. You need a look right this second?"

As if she could pull them out of her pocket, he thought.

He said, "Right about the time we get back'll be soon enough, Miss Smart Mouth."

She turned toward him, her saddle creaking softly. "Oh, is the big, bad Slocum cranky today?"

He reached over and grabbed her reins, and both horses came to a sudden halt. Loomis and his men were going to be too tired to go anywhere but straight home, which was in the other direction, so he didn't have them to worry about. But Maddie was pouring oil on a fire that had been smoldering and smoking ever since he'd handed his horse over to pull that damn travois full of Basque shepherd.

"I've had a horseshit day, if you gotta know," he growled. "I had to walk for half of it, and these boots I got on ain't made for travelin' shank's mare. Your buddy Loomis showed up with a few of his boys, and there was a . . . a little hoorah with him. I've been riding—and I mention it again in case you missed it the first time, *walking*—behind a bunch of smelly sheep all day, and then I come back to find you run off to who knows where. Yes," he answered her snidely, mimicking her tone of voice, "Slocum is cranky as a bastard."

"Loomis showed up?" she asked, ignoring the rest of his tale of woe. "Why, that ring-tailed son-ofabitch!"

"And if you hadn't kited out on your own," Slocum said, "you could have called him that to his face."

"You brought him back?" she said, surprised. "To the ranch? To *my* ranch?"

"Walked him in," he said. "Smack dab in the middle of a flock of sheep."

She began to laugh. And actually, when he thought about Loomis in the middle of those wool-lies, with the old ram giving him a shove about every twentieth step, it did seem pretty funny.

But he held himself down to a sideways grin, and said, "Maddie? Damn it, Maddie, stop laughing. You shouldn't have taken off by yourself. Don't do it again, or I swear, I'll turn you over my knee."

Still giggling, she said, "Promise?"

"Maddie!"

"You can turn me over your knee any time, Slocum, and I'm going to give you just cause," she bubbled.

Women. He didn't have the slightest idea what she was talking about. "You sunstroked, woman?"

She reached behind her, fumbling with one of the saddlebags. "No, not hardly, you big, dumb, adorable saddle tramp." She brought out a hand, curled into a fist. "We thought Daddy mined out all the gold, you know? We thought it was all used up. He thought so too. But guess what I found today."

She opened her fist, and in the dying sunlight, Slocum saw the rock she held. It glimmered slightly. Quartz, shot through with gold streaks.

He thumbed back his hat. "Well, I'll be double-dogged."

"We'll have to have it assayed, of course. I mean, it could turn out to be nothing but pyrite crystals—fool's gold. But if it's as rich as I think it is . . ."

"Where the hell'd you find this?" he asked, taking the small rock from her. "I thought you were certain this land was all played out."

"Apparently not. At least, I hope not. This morning, after you left, while we were mixing the adobe, Mike started rambling on about Apache Canyon. That's on my land, up to the northeast corner of the spread. Anyway, he was going on about how some of Loomis's cattle had wandered down as far as Apache Canyon last March, and how they'd had to go down to get them.''

"I thought Loomis's cattle were all up in the high country," he said. "Haven't seen so much as a dried-up cow chip.''

"They're in the mountains, all right," she said a little testily. "But about two dozen head wandered down last winter. There was late snow up in the Bradshaws, and I guess they got lost or something. Will you let me finish?''

He nodded.

"Anyway," she went on, "it was just Mike and Loomis who went that day. And Mike said that Loomis's horse pulled up lame while they were down there, in the canyon. Loomis picked a rock out of its hoof, and Mike said he started acting strange. Told him not to mention it to anybody. Which he didn't, until just this morning.''

Slocum handed the rock back to her, but held silent.

She shook her head. Holding the rock up to catch the last rays of the sun, she said, "That poor kid's about as smart as a box of dirt, isn't he?''

Slocum waited for her to get to the point.

"The funny thing was, Loomis didn't throw that rock away, like anybody else would," she continued. She slipped the rock back in her saddlebag and gave the flap a pat. "No, he stared at it for quite a long time, spat on it and rubbed it with his fingers, and then he stuck it in his pocket. And right after, he started trying to get rid of me. Us, I should say. And started building his stupid whorehouse.''

Slocum said, ''Mike told you this?''

''Not at first,'' she answered. ''Only the part about Loomis's horse going lame in Apache Canyon. I asked him why—only to be conversational, you understand. Well, all right, to get him to talk about *anything* besides Charity. Listening to any man, even poor, dumb Mike, go on for hours about some other woman isn't my favorite thing.''

He grinned at her. ''Vanity, thy name is Maddie,'' he said, quoting from somebody or other.

''Hmph,'' she snorted. ''For your information, Charity isn't interested in the slightest. Wish Mike'd get that through his thick skull, but he's as pigheaded as Mace. Must run in the family. And can we get moving now? My stomach's growling. It wants some of Jane's biscuits and my own beef ragout.''

''Hope that means stew,'' he said as they started back toward the house. He was smiling. Maddie was a fair fancy cook, once you pinned her down to doing it. Not so fancy that you were afraid to eat it because you weren't quite sure what it was, but fancy in that she knew how to season things just right. She put together a pretty plate too, he supposed, but he didn't care about that part.

"You put the rest of it together then?" he asked. And then added, "You got that beef stew started? I mean, has it been cookin' all day?" His mouth was watering.

"Yes, on both counts." She sighed. "Lord, there isn't anything I want more than a bath and some dinner. And then . . ."

Sure of the good dinner, Slocum turned his head, waiting.

"And then," she continued, a hint of a grin creeping round the corners of her mouth, "I've been a very bad girl, Slocum, wandering out here all by myself and finding that gold. Or what looks like it anyway. But I could have been lost, or got snatched by renegades, or surrounded by Indians. I think that's exceptionally bad of me. So naughty that I think somebody might have to bend me over and paddle me on my bare bottom."

Slocum was glad it was getting dark because, as hot as his ears and neck got all of a sudden, he figured he was red as a beet.

He knew he was hard as a rock.

And he was thinking, as they rode along and he squirmed in his saddle, that there was surely nothing so good as a very bad girl.

After dinner, while Maddie soaked in the bathtub, Slocum sat behind the closed doors of Daddy O'Hara's old office, poring over the maps she'd given him.

"You'd think," he said to the Australian, who was lending a hand, "that out of all of these charts and maps and surveys, he'd have one of his own land. This book's some parcel down by Tucson."

He closed the cover and pushed it aside, and was opening another when MacGregor said, "got it!" and slid a large sheet of paper in front of him.

Slocum smiled. "This is it, all right." He ran his hands over it slowly. "Here's where we are," he said, pointing. "And here's where they were blasting where they found that first vein."

"What'd they do with all that gold anyhow?" MacGregor asked, then held up one hand. "If it's none of my business, just say the word."

"No reason why you shouldn't know," Slocum replied, tracing topographical details with his fingers. "Daddy O'Hara was a crook if there ever was one, and crazier than a rabid coyote. Planned to take over the whole of Arizona Territory and some besides, and used that gold for minting coins to pay his very own private army."

He looked up, and MacGregor's expression told him he hadn't believed a word of it.

"That's the truth," Slocum said, drawing the lantern closer. "Believe it or not."

MacGregor still didn't look convinced, and Slocum added, "MacGregor, I ain't near so good a liar as you. I can't just make up two-hundred-degree chickens on the spot. I'm tellin' the truth, okay? Daddy O'Hara had barracks down south, near Tucson, and filled 'em with volunteers. Took a whole regiment of cavalry to clear 'em out. And me. And Maddie.'' He smiled. ''Here, look. I think I got it figured.''

MacGregor, who apparently thought discretion was the better part of valor, bent over the map, following Slocum's fingers.

''Maddie's got an underground river on her land, all right,'' Slocum said, pleased with himself. ''Just like I thought. You can see where it used to run on top, where it cut canyons and gorges into the land before it went underground. That's why Maddie's got so much water that it never gives out.''

''And where's this Loomis bloke's land?'' MacGregor asked.

Slocum ran his hand across the map, to the opposite side. ''Border between the two is over here. See? She's not tapping into the Blue Calf one bit. Not even close. In fact, his river feeds hers, farther down.''

MacGregor stood up straight, grinning. ''You've got the bastard then.''

''Yeah,'' Slocum said, nodding. ''I got a feeling we're going to have to get law from someplace else to take care of it, though. Loomis has the local sheriff in his pocket. The town's only lawyer too, and he just happens to run the bank.''

''You'll be riding out then, mate? To shepherd

the legal talent?'' MacGregor looked much too eager for him to leave.

Slocum sat back in the wide chair, and grinned. ''You must've hit it off with the ladies while I was gone. Noticed Charity gave you the last ladle'a the beef stew.''

The Aussie colored a little and ducked his head. ''Aw, she was just thinkin' I was a skinny bloke, that was all. Tryin' to fatten me up.'' He patted his chest. ''Put a little meat on these bones.''

''And two slices of that layer cake?'' asked Slocum. ''And four ears of corn?''

''Same reason,'' MacGregor said indignantly. ''Why, I got bones sticking out all over!''

''And that little nudge with her hip?''

MacGregor grinned sheepishly. ''Well, all right. Doubt she thought that'd put the pounds on me.'' Then he sobered. ''Say, you ain't got . . . I mean, there's nobody what's got her marked out, is there?''

''Not me,'' said Slocum. ''But Mace's brother, Mike? He's got himself a powerful crush on her. Didn't you see him glaring at you over the table?''

''Missed that, I reckon.''

''Well, that crush'll probably wear off the minute he sees some farmer's daughter, but if I were you, I'd be careful how I handled things.''

''Mike, eh?'' MacGregor nodded. ''I'll take that into consideration.''

15

Slocum walked down the hall toward Maddie's room. She ought to be fresh as a mountain spring, for all the time she'd spent soaking in that tub. Alone, dang it. Well, he'd had to check the maps.

She'd kept her mouth shut about finding the gold too. She was a smart one, that girl, although she could have had better timing. Well, he'd just have to ride back over to Vista Verde tomorrow. It wasn't a big town and it was a day and a half's ride away, but he thought he could probably find a lawyer there that wasn't under Loomis's thumb, and a judge who'd see things his way.

He was also planning to find the assayer's office.

At Maddie's door, he rapped with his knuckles, twice.

"Mr. Slocum?" came the answer.

Mister Slocum? What was she up to now?

He opened the door to find her standing before the round table in the middle of the room, dressed in a little girl's crinolines—if that little girl had a full bust fairly falling out of the bodice, that is. Her hands were folded demurely before her, her eyes were downcast, and she was twisting one toe into the floor. All of a sudden, he knew the game she planned to play tonight.

Lord, she could make him hard faster than anything.

He closed the door behind him. And locked it.

"Hello, Maddie," he said softly. "Have you been out doin' wickedness again?"

"Yes, sir," she said, looking up at him sideways. She batted her lashes innocently. "I'm ready for someone to paddle my pink little bottom, Mr. Slocum," she said softly. And then, her voice altering to a tone more come-hither than any little girl's could ever hope to be, she added, "And after, I'll be ready for that same somebody to screw me silly."

Slocum sat down on the edge of her bed and rubbed his hands together. "Across my knees then, Miss Maddie."

She looked at him, sniffing a little, and then lay down across his lap with a rustle of fabric. "I'm sorry I was bad," she said. "Don't punish me too hard, sir."

He played along. He said, "We'll just see about that."

He took a swat at her skirts, and the force of it must have surprised her, because she turned her head and say, "Hey!"

He sank an elbow into the small of her back to pin her down, and smiled. "Damn it, I really am pissed at you, Maddie. Riding out there all by yourself!''

He whacked her again, knowing full well the force of the blow was being taken by all those petticoats. God almighty, there was a ton of them!

She was still yelping from the last blow when he said, ''You didn't tell me why that fool Loomis thought he could move you into his whorehouse either,'' and smacked her again.

''Ow!'' she cried. ''You didn't ask!''

''Yes, I did.'' The hand came down again.

''Slocum, stop it! And I didn't tell you because it was all so stupid, that's all.''

Again, the flat of his hand struck layers of fabric.

''Ooo, you stinker, you! Well, who wants to admit that they're being terrorized by some idiot who can't even—''

Somebody knocked at the door, and they both froze. MacGregor's voice came through the planks. ''Everything, um, all right in there?''

As one, Slocum and Maddie said, ''Yes,'' and then Slocum added, ''Go away!''

''Sorry,'' said the voice, and then MacGregor's footsteps retreated down the hall.

''You're so forceful, darlin','' Maddie said, and batted her lashes.

''You don't know the half of it,'' he replied, and lifted her skirts.

Sure enough, once he got through folding back

all those layers of petticoats, there was nothing between him and that sweet, pink fanny but air. Gently, he laid his big hand on the exposed flesh, and beneath his palm, he felt Maddie shudder.

When he didn't move, Maddie's voice, very small, said, "I hope you're not still mad, Slocum. Because if you are, I'm going to call MacGregor back again."

He squeezed her pretty little backside, then gave each cheek a playful slap. "What? And make me share? I don't think so, Miss Maddie. You'll take your punishment and you'll like it."

He moved his elbow, releasing her, but she didn't get up. Instead, she wriggled onto her back. She hiked the front of her skirt too, hiked up all those petticoats, until they were pooled at her waist and her front—at least, from the waist down—was as bare and exposed as her backside had been, and then she took his hand and tucked it high between her legs.

"Yes, sir," she said demurely. "Punish me."

She guided his hand, showing his fingers where to go—as if they didn't already know the way. "Make me crazy, Slocum."

But he stood up, and Maddie went tumbling to the floor.

"Hey!" she said, plainly annoyed. "What the hell do you think you're doing?"

"Honey," he said, propping his elbows on his knees and wiping at his brow—and trying not to think about his erection, "first, I want some answers. Some straight ones. Seems every time I get around to asking, you bulldog me by wavin' your fanny in my face."

"I could wave my tits more often if you like," she replied.

"Maddie, be serious for a half a second. Why didn't you tell me about this harebrained scheme of Loomis's?"

She snorted and gathered her skirts about her. "I already told you. Because nothing could come of it. Because it was, well, embarrassing, him thinking he could do that in this day and age, even if he could prove his silly water rights claim, which he can't. We're not touching his precious water. Daddy said it was an artesian well."

Slocum shook his head. "You've got to learn to do your homework, Maddie. It's not a well."

"It isn't?"

"No."

She held out her hand for some help up, but he just let her sit there, on the floor. She folded her arms and lifted her lip in a mock snarl.

"What it is," he continued, "is an underground river. It's totally divorced from the stream Loomis claims you're using—and the one Daddy O'Hara and your real father before him used for the last couple of decades."

"Oh," she said, and crossed her arms. "Well, then, there you are."

He sighed. "Maddie, what would you have done if I hadn't come riding in here? You couldn't prove it, not without checking those maps, and not without a lawyer, which seems to be a commodity that there ain't any of except Loomis's. Did you even think of those maps? With his connections, Loomis could'a got you thrown out eventually, if you never thought to check, if you kept on trying to solve this thing by the sheer force of your own will."

She set her jaw. "I've got my own way of dealing with things."

"Gee," Slocum said sarcastically, "and your way has worked real well so far. Let's see now. One dead hired gun, one burned barn, stray bullets flying all over—"

"Oh, shut up."

He grabbed her arm and pulled her up beside him, on the bed. "Honey," he said, cupping the point of her elbow in his hand, "there are some things you can't just bull your way through."

She didn't look at him, preferring, it seemed, to glare straight ahead. "Always worked before."

He moved his hand up her arm, to her shoulder. "There's a first time for everything. And a second, probably."

Now she was staring at her lap.

"Just promise me that you'll tell me everything that threatens you from now on," he said. "Even if you think it's stupid, even if you think it's lamebrained, even if you think it couldn't affect you in a million years. Promise?"

She didn't answer.

"Maddie, promise me," he said gently. "I worry about you, damn it."

She looked up, peering sideways, and in a tiny voice said, "You do?"

He cupped her chin in his hand then, and lifted it until she was turned toward him. "Maddie O'Hara," he said softly, "you are the damnedest woman west of the Mississippi. You're resourceful and smart and gutsy and brave, not to mention the best piece of ass this ol' cowboy's ever had. But sometimes you just take it too dang far. When I tell you I worry about you, it's no lie. Hell, I think about you practically the whole day long."

She smiled, just a little. "I know men. You mean that you think about me when I'm around."

"Well," he admitted, "sometimes when I'm not around you too. Hell, I rode clear out from California to visit you, didn't I?"

"Two years after we last said good-bye."

He sighed. There was no way he was going to win this one. He said, "Stop shovin' the subject around, all right? Let's just leave it that all in all, Maddie O'Hara, you are one all-consumin' subject. I don't want anything bad to happen to you."

And then he felt her small hand slipping toward his crotch.

"Have I told you, Slocum," she said, "that

you're the sweetest man I know?'' And then, with a smile, she added, ''That I know this week anyhow.''

Just like that, his fading erection was back, full force. She began to slowly unbutton his britches, saying, ''You think you could make love to me real slow? I'm out of the mood for games. Make love to me, Slocum,'' she said, freeing him at last. ''Make love to me like you mean it, like maybe I was some fresh-faced little farm girl and you loved me.''

''I do love you, Maddie,'' he whispered, and at that moment, he truly meant it.

He helped her out of her dress, she helped him out of his clothes, and then he blew out the light and loved her long and soft and slow, as if they were both young and tender and unscarred by life.

As if they were both innocent.

16

Two days later, Mr. J. Aldritch Foxworthy, the only attorney in Vista Verde who hadn't left his office for the day, set aside the papers Slocum had brought, and which he'd been poring over for the last half hour.

He sat back in his chair, folded his hands over his considerable belly, and said, "Gracious sakes alive. Seems this fellow's been readin' his law books upside down and drunk."

Slocum smiled. "Figured you'd say that."

"Indeed, indeed," replied Foxworthy. "Any fool can see he's got no claim whatsoever to her water. Although it goes without saying that the question's vice versa. I mean, that she has no claim on his water either. She's not accessing it, there's no question?"

"No question."

"Of course, if he intends to push the issue, you could end up—that is, Miss O'Hara could end up—in court for some time. These things tend to draw out, you know. Oh, don't get me wrong. She'd win, particularly if I were the attorney on the case," he added, somewhat pompously, "but there'd be time spent and legal fees, ad nauseam."

"I'm sure there would," muttered Slocum. He didn't much care for Foxworthy's profession. Bunch of fancy bloodsuckers, if you asked him. Come to think of it, he wouldn't have liked Foxworthy if he were a bartender, and that just happened to be one of Slocum's favorite professions.

"Yes," Foxworthy continued happily, oblivious to Slocum's distrust. "It could end up costing her a very pretty penny indeed."

Slocum stood up. "I'd appreciate it if you could get those legal wheels in motion, Mr. Foxworthy. The sooner the better."

Foxworthy remained seated. "Certainly, Mr. Slocum, certainly. I'll file an injunction first thing, and have the papers ready for you by noon. Just being served with them ought to settle Mr. Loomis's hash."

"Who's gonna serve them?" Slocum asked. He settled his hat on his head. "I told you about the sheriff."

Foxworthy waved a thick hand. "Don't fear, sir. I'm going to have you declared a temporary officer of the court. Well, Judge Thibodeaux will do the swearing in. It will enable you to serve Loomis the papers yourself. But that's all," he added, raising one brow. "Don't go getting any grandiose ideas."

In spite of himself, Slocum grinned.

"Meet me at the courthouse at noon, sir," Fox-

. worthy went on, "and we'll get this whole thing taken care of." He shook his head. "It's a very good thing that you came to me, Mr. Slocum."

Slocum figured he was talking about the legal fee, which Slocum was certain would go right to Foxworthy's belly, but the lawyer said, "Those ladies could have been in quite a speck of trouble, what with that antiquated Batista law still on the books."

Slocum squinted. "The what?"

"Batista law," Foxworthy said. "Laws actually." He seemed delighted to have found an audience to amaze. "Old Spanish stuff. Well, not Spanish exactly. Can't remember just when it came on the books. Well before my time, though."

"And what's it say exactly?"

"Simply speaking, that if Person A owes a debt to Person B," Foxworthy explained, "Person A may be forced into labor at the discretion of Person B, for so long as it takes said debt to be resolved."

Slocum was silent for a moment. "You're foolin' me."

"Just as I said, Mr. Slocum." With a creak of his chair, Foxworthy sat forward. "No joke. And since there are no specific statutes banning prostitution in the Territory, and this obscure law states that the labor be at the discretion of the party harmed . . ." He shrugged his shoulders.

In the space of a few minutes, Slocum's whole

attitude about the legal profession had been proven sound, but his opinion of this particular practitioner of it had risen considerably. He said, "I'll be damned. Whatever you're charging, Mr. Foxworthy, it ain't enough."

"Hmph," said the lawyer. "We'll see if you still say that when I hand you my bill. Now go." He flicked a hand, wiggling the fingers. "Shoo. Get along with you. My wife's roasting a pork loin tonight."

After dropping by the livery to check on Bess, he walked up the street to McMahon's Grill. There was a fair-sized crowd coming and going.

The crowd coming out was smiling, so he figured the food should be all right. And since he hadn't stuck around town last time long enough for anybody to connect him as the buyer of MacGregor's sheep, he also figured to be safe on moral grounds. Cattlemen's morals, that was.

On the other hand, he thought with a grin as he entered the restaurant, maybe he should have introduced himself as the man who'd taken the last sheep out of Vista Verde. Maybe they'd have thrown him a party.

As was his habit, he picked a table in back, next to the wall, and sat against it so that he could see the whole room while he ate. He studied the chalkboard menu on the wall across the room, and when the waiter arrived, he ordered a beer and a big steak, charred, with fried potatoes and fried onions, with a cheese and pepper quesadilla on the side.

"Dessert?" the waiter said over the noise of the room, his pencil poised.

"Reckon I'll figure that out later," he said, and the waiter went away.

By the time the quesadilla and the beer arrived, he had gotten over the desire to throttle Loomis, or at least temporarily pushed it to the back burner. He dove into the quesadilla. He hadn't realized how hungry he was, and as he quickly devoured the tortilla, sandwiched with grilled green peppers and fried cheese, he wondered if maybe he ought to order up a second steak.

The idea disappeared when the rest of his dinner arrived, however. The steak was still sizzling, and so big that it covered the place entirely and hung off the sides. The fried potatoes and onions, smelling of salt and fat and tickling at his nose, took up a second plate.

"Anything else, sir?" the waiter said.

"For right now, just bring me the ketchup," he said, reaching for the salt and pepper. He went to work on the steak.

Sometime later, after his dishes were cleared and he was paused in the middle of his apple pie, wondering if he could finish it, somebody across the room shouted, "Hey, Slocum!"

His hand was halfway to his gun when he recognized the man who'd shouted, and who was making his way across the crowded room to Slocum's table.

Slocum stood up and pulled the napkin from his collar. "Peabody?" he said, suddenly as happy as all get-out. "Rance Peabody? Well, I'll be a ring-tailed sonofabitch!"

"Not just on my account, I hope," Rance said, reaching him at last. They shook hands and pounded each other's backs.

"Sit down, you old badger's butt!" Slocum said happily. "Pull up a chair!" He hadn't seen Rance Peabody for something like six years, not since the trouble up on the Platt River. "By God! I thought you were dead!"

"Heard the same about you, you old skunk!" Rance said, laughing. "Heard you took a bullet to the lung out in California and croaked."

"A small exaggeration," replied Slocum, smiling at the tall, lanky redhead. As always, he looked like he'd just come straight from either the bathhouse or the barbershop. "I took the bullet, all right, but I was only half-killed. I heard you went down on the Brazos."

"A bald-faced lie," Rance replied, waving at the waiter. "I went down on the Brazos, all right, but not down *in* it. Floated with the current for six miles and got fished out by a dazzler of a Mexican woman, name of Carmen Lopez, who fixed me up. In more ways than one," he added with a wink.

He ordered a beer for himself and a refill for

Slocum, and confided, "They're always dazzlers when they pull you out of the water, ain't they? Hell's bells, I must've swallowed a whole wagonload of mud and fish shit! If'n I never see the Brazos again, it'll be too soon to suit me."

The beers arrived, Slocum rolled himself a quirlie, and the two men caught up on old times. Seemed that of late, Rance was hiring his gun out, and he wasn't letting it go cheap.

"Hell's bells!" he said, stroking his red mustache. Like his hair, it was shot through with gray, and Slocum realized that Rance must be pushing fifty. "I ain't so young anymore, you know. If I'm gonna go gun somebody, I oughta get paid for it, and paid good. I'm lookin' to retire next year."

Slocum snorted. Fifty or no, the Rance Peabody he knew was destined to die in the saddle or at the business end of a bullet, not sipping some fancy drink in some hotel lobby.

"Retire? You? That's a laugh!"

"Naw, Slocum," he said, shaking his head. "I mean it. Reflexes are slowing down. Hell, they been slowin' down since I hit forty. Thought maybe I'd buy me a place and raise me some cattle. Maybe horses. Get genteel."

"Rance Peabody, a gentleman?" Slocum said, laughing. "Next thing I know, you'll be wantin' to take a wife!"

Rance smiled and leaned back in his chair. "Thought about that too."

Slocum shook his head. "Well, I'll be double-dogged."

"You shouldn't be smoking them horseshit things," Rance said suddenly, as if he had just noticed Slocum's quirlie. He dug into his breast pocket and produced a long silver case. "Put that out and try one'a these," he said, opening it to reveal three fat cigars. They were expensive too, by the look of them.

"You don't have to ask me twice," Slocum said, taking one and running it under his nose, capturing the sweet, musky scent. They were Havanas, all right. He bit off the end and lit it. It was past fine, maybe even better than the late Daddy O'Hara's stock, back at the ranch.

"So what brings you to Vista Verde?" Rance asked through a yellow-white haze of cigar smoke. He lit one up too.

"Takin' care of some business for a friend," Slocum replied. He didn't see the need to go into details. "And you?"

"Just travelin' through," Rance said. He paused to take a draw on his beer. "Got a job to do over to Three Wives."

Suddenly, the cigar tasted rancid in Slocum's mouth. He could only think of one man that would be hiring. "Three Wives?"

"Yeah." Rance cocked his head. "Heard of it?"

"I have. You wouldn't be goin' down there to

work for a fella named Loomis, would you?''

Rance's brows bunched. "Yeah. Why?"

Slocum slouched back in his chair. Just when he thought he had the threads of this damn thing half straightened out, they'd gone and got ten all tangled up again.

"Shit," he muttered. "Rance, I think we need to get out of this restaurant. Let's take ourselves up the street to the saloon for some serious drinking. I got a real long story to tell you."

Two hours and innumerable whiskeys later, Rance leaned his elbow on a rear table down at the Double Eagle Saloon, and slurred, "Hell's bells, Slocum! It all comes down to the dang female population. They're nothin' but trouble. Yessir."

"Bet your ass," said Slocum, who was equally soused. He went to prop his elbow on the table and parrot Rance's move, but he missed and hit his knee instead.

"See?" crowed Rance drunkenly. "Females did that to you! Female women!"

"Can't live with 'em," Slocum said as he finally succeeded in sitting back in his chair, which he'd been trying to find the middle of for the last fifteen minutes.

"Can't live without 'em," said Rance philosophically, and fell straight forward, onto the tabletop, dead to the world.

Slocum sighed heavily, and blearily studied his

friend, now snoring on the table. Seemed like Slocum wasn't the only one who'd lost his hollow leg with the passing years. He could remember a time when Rance would have drunk as much before breakfast, and still gone out and shot a silver dollar dead center at twenty paces.

Well, maybe fifteen.

He realized, as he pushed himself to his feet and wobbled round the table, that they were both going to pay for this in the morning. But it'd be worth it if he had Rance on his side.

Of course, he wasn't entirely clear just where Rance stood on the matter. About halfway into the second bottle, Rance had stopped venturing opinions and instead, taken to slurring, "Damn females!" over and over.

Rance hadn't confided where he was staying, so Slocum heaved him up, tucked him clumsily under his arm, and wobbled out of the saloon and down the street, toward his own hotel.

Rance seemed to have grown considerably heavier since their last meeting.

By the time they'd passed the assayer's office where Slocum had left his ore sample earlier in the afternoon, Rance was so heavy that Slocum was forced to drop him in the street and take a breather.

And by the time that he picked him up again and wove his way to the hotel, Rance had gotten so heavy that he had to get the desk clerk to help move him up the stairs. And the desk clerk had to get two boys to help *him*.

Well, they were pushing Slocum up there too.

Slocum woke with a ringing head, a rocky stomach, and a sick feeling that this wasn't going to be one of his favorite days.

The upholstered chair across the room was full of a snoring and sprawled Rance Peabody, and the first thing Slocum did—once he could stand up and walk, that is—was to give Rance a good kick.

Rance fell out of the chair, and his gun cleared leather before he hit the floor, tumbling. Fortunately for Slocum, he looked before he pulled the trigger.

"Oh," he said, and he looked cranky as a bear who'd been awakened in midwinter by mice gnawing on his toes. "It's you." He reholstered his gun, squinted at the window, and gripped his head in both hands. "It just me, or is that a terrible bright moon?"

"It's nigh on ten o'clock in the morning," Slocum grumbled. "Lord, Rance, I never heard nobody snore as loud as you."

From beneath his hands, which were gripped to his face, Rance said, "You think that's loud, you sonofabitch, you oughta hear me fart."

After they tidied themselves up and shaved—somewhat shakily—they eventually found their way downstairs. Rance, who had cleaned up pretty good, all things considered, allowed as how he'd like a bite of breakfast.

Slocum, who was still of a mind to bite the head off anybody who said "hello" to him the wrong way, declined. "Got some things to take care of," he said. "Meet me at the livery at half past noon. Beats me how you can even think about vittles."

"Hmph," grunted Rance. "I sure hope you're in a human mood by then. A half-dozen eggs and a rasher of bacon'd do you good."

Slocum's stomach turned over at the thought of it, but Rance went on blithely. "I don't much favor the idea of puttin' my behind in the saddle for fifty-some miles with a cuss that's bitchin' 'cause his horse is breathin' too loud. Makes for a right borin' conversation."

Slocum growled, "Just be there." And to the painful sound of Rance's laughter, he started up the street, headed for the assayer's office.

He'd left the rock Maddie showed him, along with three others she'd picked up in the same place, and the news was better than he could have hoped for: high-grade ore.

The other strike had been downstream, and it had been a vein. This gold, completely divorced in source from the first paydirt, was along the same underground riverbed, but it had washed down from someplace higher up. Probably not quite the quality that Daddy O'Hara had been stealing out from under Maddie's pretty little nose, but sure as hell worth scooping up.

Or in Loomis's case, stealing.

Slocum paid, took the assayer's report, and made his way to the town courthouse. Foxworthy met him on the steps.

"Take your damn hat off, Slocum," he grumbled as they went inside. "It's full of holes."

"Only two," Slocum growled.

"Take it off."

Slocum was duly deputized—for the delivery of the papers only, both Judge Thibodeaux and Lawyer Foxworthy stressed repeatedly—and left with a manilla envelope tucked under his arm.

Foxworthy accompanied him halfway to the hotel, and said in parting, "Take care of yourself, Slocum. Get a new hat. And let me know how this thing of yours turns out."

"If it don't turn out right," Slocum said, pressing a hand to his still-aching temple, "I reckon you'll be hearing from somebody, all right."

Rance was waiting at the livery, his big liver-chestnut gelding already groomed to a spit-polish sheen and tacked up in a tooled saddle, set with silver. Rance hadn't changed a lick since the last time Slocum had seen him.

And breakfast must have agreed with him. He gave the appearance of having slept ten hours the night before, and looked as if he'd never so much as seen a bottle of whiskey, let alone put one away single-handed.

Mumbling to himself, Slocum led his own mare out of her stall and began to give her a cursory going-over with the curry and brush.

"What did you do?" Slocum asked as he worked. "You got yourself a bunch of pixies on the payroll, all scramblin' ahead of you to make things pretty?"

"Only three," Rance said, straight-faced. "And I favor leprechauns myself."

Slocum grunted.

"Get your business taken care of?"

Slocum grunted again. He hadn't mentioned the gold and he wasn't going to, at least not until he was sure which side Rance was on. He put the brushes down and started tacking up Bess.

"I can see I'm gonna really enjoy this ride," Rance went on while Slocum slung the saddle up over Bess's back.

Rance leaned against the side of the livery and polished his nails on his sleeve. "Ain't often I get to travel with a true conversational genius. How's the trail anyway?"

Slocum paused, waiting for Bess to let out her breath, and said, "It's an easy ride, and there's potable water about twenty miles out. Ought to make it in two days." He looked at the sky, squinting up—somewhat less painfully than he had an hour ago—into the clear, blue-white brightness of it. "Day and a half, if the weather holds."

"Oh, joy," Rance said, and swung a leg up over his chestnut. With all that silver trimming and the spit and polish, he always looked to Slocum as if he was going out to lead a parade instead of kill somebody.

Slocum mounted Bess, and as he reined her around, Rance said, "Say, ain't you gonna get you a new hat while you're in town? Didn't want to mention it last night, but you're in dire need, boy!"

17

Maddie quietly opened her door and made her way down the darkened hallway. Funny how she couldn't sleep without Slocum in her bed. Funny how she'd been just fine until he showed up, and how she couldn't seem to do without him now.

She padded along the hall, out into the main room, and headed for the kitchen and the pump. A glass of water might be all she needed to settle her down.

A glass of water instead of a man?

Well, she supposed she'd better get used to it. Slocum wasn't a man to linger long in any one place. Never had been, never would be. He'd be moving on one day.

At the big dining table that marked the division between the kitchen and the living room, she paused. Voices, engaged in conversation. Listening, she identified one of them as Jane. The other voice, a man's, wasn't so easy to peg.

Jane? Alone with a man, without taking an ax to him? This was certainly a new development. Despite her profession, Jane hadn't been any too keen on the male sex when Maddie left Chicago two years ago. A year later, when Maddie had sent for Jane and Charity, Jane had seemed worse, if that were possible.

Amoral by design, Maddie had relished her work in the gaming house—albeit with certain exceptions. Charity hadn't been as enthusiastic as Maddie—well, who had?—but she surely did appreciate the finer things in life, things that could only be gotten with the high fees she brought.

But Jane? She'd merely gone through the motions. She smiled when it was time to smile, she laughed when it was time to laugh, and she spread her legs when it was time for that. She did her work with precision and a somewhat feigned delight, and a certain degree of ingenuity and flair—the house demanded that—but never once did she seem to take any pleasure in it.

Maddie had never asked Jane about her past life, before she'd landed at the whorehouse in Chicago. And unlike many of the other girls—who couldn't keep their mouths shut if you paid them—Jane hadn't offered any information. Maddie had guessed, at the time, that something in that past was pretty awful, which was why she'd never pressed her.

But if she wasn't hearing things, there was Jane, the confirmed man-hater—the man-*gutter,* given half a chance—out on the front porch in the middle of the night, talking in a civilized fashion to a bona fide male of the species.

Would wonders never cease? Had she fallen for Mace's dubious charms at last? After all, he hadn't come a-singing tonight. Maybe the lack of sour notes had softened her up.

Maddie crept toward the front window, feeling her way as she went. Her basic nature made her incapable of passing up an opportunity to eavesdrop, to find out who Jane was having this little midnight confabulation with.

And then she stopped stock-still.

She knew that voice, and it sure wasn't Mace.

It was Ed Barlow, Loomis's right-hand man.

Maddie felt as if she were drowning in the darkness as she heard Jane say, "He'd better make good on his word. He doesn't, and he's going to be sorry. You tell him that."

Barlow's voice answered, "I reckon he knows that, Jane, but you sure drive a hard bargain. He's just tryin' to be like family and, well, what with y'all bein' whores and all, that's a mighty big stretch. If it was me, I'd—"

"Well, it's not you, is it?" Jane interrupted curtly, then spat, "Family, my sweet Aunt Fanny! Oh, I'd love to hear what he told you was goin' on. Some fairy tale, I'll bet. And family? That slimy goat-sucker doesn't know the meaning of the word. Listen, I did everything I promised so far. The next move is yours. Now go on, get the hell out of here before somebody sees you."

Chairs scraped outside, and Maddie heard the

sound of a horse's hooves walking away over the soft dust of the yard. Shivering with anger, she sat down at the table and waited for Jane.

But Jane didn't come inside. Maddie counted to ten—three times—and managed to get her anger under control—at least for the moment—but there was still no Jane to be seen.

"What'd you do, Jane?" she asked the darkness. "Sneak in and out of your window, like some lovesick sixteen-year-old?"

"I was waiting for you to come out," came the unexpected reply from the porch. She'd been positive Jane was gone by this time. "Eavesdropping works both ways, Maddie. And since we still have no glass in the windows, we might as well be in the same room, so far as the sound carrying goes. Thought I heard somebody come down the hall. Knew for certain I heard somebody sit down. That chair squeaks. Come on out."

"I'm too mad to be on the same porch with you, Jane," Maddie said through clenched teeth. She guessed all that counting-to-ten business hadn't worked as well as she'd thought. "What are you doing to me? You selling me out? Ann-Elizabeth might have run out on us, but at least she only took a buckboard. You're taking my land!"

"I'm just causing you a mite of inconvenience, that's all," came the answer, and calmer than Maddie had expected. "A tiny bit of inconvenience for you will buy a pound of justice for me."

"What the hell are you talking about, Jane? Why were you cozied up with Ed Barlow? You hate Ed Barlow!"

A sigh came from the porch, a sigh carried on the breeze that fluttered the curtains and washed cool over Maddie's cheek. "You have to trust me," Jane said. "Please trust me for a little while longer?"

Maddie's hands balled into fists on the tabletop. "I oughta get the shotgun, that's what I oughta do. Damn you anyway!" She paused, trying to regain control of herself. After a moment, she exhaled loudly and said, "Jane?"

There came a sigh, echoing hers, and then Jane snapped, "What?"

"I've seen you shoot quite a bit since you came out here with Charity. You're a good shot, maybe the best I've ever seen, male or female."

"A freak of nature, that's all," Jane replied, and along with curiosity, there was a note of pride in her voice. "If it holds still long enough, I can shoot the buzz off a fly. Why bring it up now?"

"Was that you?" Maddie asked the darkness. "Shooting at my Slocum those times, I mean. I don't seem to remember you being around the ranch either time."

There was a long pause, and Maddie expected her to say that Geraldo had been absent both times as well—which he had—and blame it on him.

But instead, after a moment, Jane said, "Now

you're calling him 'my Slocum'?'' Then she snorted. ''Jesus, Maddie, I didn't hurt him. I was just tryin' to scare him off.''

''You could have killed him!'' Maddie said, not understanding. ''Just a half inch and—''

''But I didn't, did I?'' Jane replied.

Maddie closed her eyes. ''I suppose it wouldn't do any good to ask why?''

''No more than it would do me any good to ask why you're so goddamn fond of that old rooster,'' Jane said curtly.

And then, taking no care to disguise the disgust in her voice, Jane added, ''Ever since he got here, it's been Slocum this and Slocum that, and the two of you goin' at it morning, noon, and night—not to mention every spare second in between—like you were a couple'a yowlin' barn cats. If you were getting paid half of what you used to get, you could'a retired by now and bought yourself a yacht!''

''Just a little one,'' Maddie said impatiently. ''And stop trying to change the subject. Friendship only goes so far, Jane, and I'm not certain it goes far enough to make me pretend I didn't hear any of what you and Ed Barlow said out there on my own porch. I think I've got a right to—''

She stopped at the unmistakable sound of a gunshot, echoing thinly in the distance, and stood up. Her chair toppled behind her, but she paid it no mind. As quickly as she could, she groped her way to the door.

It was a good bit easier to see things once she was outside, with no roof between her and the moon. The first thing she saw was Jane, already at the porch rail and staring out to the southwest, toward the pastures where Taggart MacGregor and Miguel had moved their woolly charges.

"There," Jane said, pointing. "It came from over there."

Just as Maddie opened her mouth to answer, another shot split the night. "My flock," she whispered over the high, streaking sound of its echo.

And then she turned on Jane, shouting, "Is this part of your secret? To sic that trash, Ed Barlow, on my flock? Did you set fire to my barn too? Of all the ungrateful, spiteful bitches!"

"Let's just watch who's calling who a bitch," Jane fairly snarled. "And it's not Ed doing the shooting, you little fool."

Suddenly all business, she snugged a shawl over her robe, then pushed Maddie out of her path. "Ed went the other way. And I don't know about you, but I'm riding out to the flock."

She headed for the corral and the horses, and Maddie, confused but still mad as a riled badger, was hot on her heels.

"A coyote?" Maddie said again through her chattering teeth. "You shot at a coyote?"

"That's the size of it," MacGregor replied, grinning, his eyes flicking to her chest.

"I'll thank you to keep your eyes up here on my face, Mr. MacGregor," she snapped, suddenly aware that she'd ridden out here in nothing but a cotton nightgown. At least Jane, who stood silently beside her, had on a robe as well as a shawl.

He touched the brim of his funny little cap. "Sorry 'bout that, ma'am. You appear to be a bit on the chilly side, though."

She looked down, then hurriedly crossed her arms over her chest. "Can we get back to coyote-shooting, please? Why didn't you just send one of these dogs out after it?"

She pointed to the three dogs, placidly lounging beside MacGregor's campfire, their tongues lolling despite the chill.

"Oh, that wouldn't have done at all," he said in his odd accent, shaking his head. "Coyotes're tricky. Why, if I'd sent one'a my dogs out after it, there might've been a whole pack of the critters just lyin' in wait, ready to rip her to shreds. As is it," he said, pointing to the fresh coyote carcass hanging from the dropping limb of a stunted palo verde, "I still got all my dogs, and Miguel here is gonna have himself a new fur vest."

Behind him, in the glow of the campfire, the Basque shepherd nodded and grinned wide, exposing a gap where his two front teeth should have been, and the soft glint of a gold eyetooth.

"Don't suppose Miss Charity came along with you?" MacGregor asked, hopefully searching the night beyond the fire.

"No," Maddie said, and MacGregor's disappointed expression wasn't lost on her. Sweet on little Charity, was he? "I doubt it made enough noise to wake the others."

She'd gotten over most of her anger at him for scaring her, but she still had plenty to spare for Jane, as well as for Geraldo, who was supposedly on guard. Nobody'd seen hide nor hair of him since supper.

She put a bare foot into her stirrup and hoisted herself up into the saddle. "Come on, Jane," she said curtly, even though her teeth were chattering to beat the band. "I think you and I have still got a few things to talk about."

MacGregor caught her rein. "Here," he said, handing something up. "At least take this. You look like you're freezin', and sound like it too. Besides, it ain't exactly fittin' for you to be . . ." His eyes flicked to her leg, bared to mid-thigh.

Annoyed, she snatched at the offered item, and found that it was a blanket, and a fairly clean one at that.

"Um . . . thank you," she said in surprise, and pulled it around her. Sweet on little Titian-haired Charity, back at the house, and giving the blanket to *her*. Was it possible that their rough and rowdy Mr. MacGregor was secretly a gentleman?

They all turned their heads at the sound of approaching hoofbeats.

"Don't shoot," called Geraldo well before they saw him, and it was only than that she realized that Miguel had produced a rifle from beneath his blankets, and MacGregor had eased the biggest knife she'd ever seen from his boot.

"Geraldo?" MacGregor answered, suddenly grinning. He put his knife away, although Miguel held the rifle steady. "C'mon in, you old pelican!"

Only when Geraldo rode into the firelight—and did so decidedly alone—did Miguel quietly slip the rifle back where it came from.

Geraldo tipped his sombrero to Maddie and Jane. "I hear the shots," he explained. "I was far." He pointed back toward the other side of the ranch house, out toward the site of the old diggings. "I come as soon as I can."

"It's all right, Geraldo," Maddie said, gathering her reins. "Just our sheep men, shooting at a coyote." She tipped her head toward the carcass. "And killing it."

"Ah," said Geraldo, with obvious admiration. "The pelt, she would make a fine vest."

MacGregor said, "That's just what we was thinkin'. Reckon it gets cold enough to freeze the bill off a platypus out here, come winter."

"Oh, *sí*!" Geraldo replied, nodding eagerly. "Well, *sí* if you would tell me what a platypus is. But I remember one time it got so cold that—"

"Jesus Christ!" said Maddie, and the men, star-tled—and possibly shocked, although she was too annoyed to figure that one out—looked up.

"Can we save the chitchat for later?" she went on. "For instance, when it's not past midnight? Geraldo, you get back to doing whatever it is you do. Mr. MacGregor, you and Miguel do the same. Jane, we have things to discuss."

But Geraldo said, "Señorita Maddie?"

She gritted her teeth. "What?"

"There is something you should know."

"And that is?"

Geraldo shrugged. "That I caught Ed Barlow riding on our land. I hit him on the head pretty good." He smirked. "You know, that one, he is one dumb hombre. I hear him coming from far off, and he rides right under the tree I am hiding in! You know the one, the big ironwood beside the trail that leads down to where we dug the—"

"Geraldo!" Maddie shouted in exasperation. "Where is he now?"

"I tie him up underneath that same tree he rides under, Señorita," Geraldo replied. He appeared to be slightly insulted by the question.

"Go back and untie him," Jane said. It was the first thing she'd said since they left the ranch house, and if Maddie wasn't hearing things—which was entirely possible at this stage in the game—she detected a note of hysteria in her voice. Odd.

Firmly, Maddie said, "You'll do no such thing, Geraldo."

"Do it, Geraldo," Jane insisted, and then she gave Maddie a pleading look.

It was a first. Maddie had never before known Jane to ask for a favor. She'd never before known Jane to ask for anything, for that matter, whether it was owed to her or not. And at that moment, that single beseeching expression touched Maddie's heart more deeply than any thoughts of losing the ranch could touch her anger.

"Do as Miss Jane says, Geraldo," Maddie heard herself say. She was still looking at Jane, and saw her face soften and sag with relief and gratitude. "Turn him loose."

"Señorita Maddie? You mean let him go?"

"Yes."

Softly, Jane said, "Thank you."

"Señorita?"

Maddie's head snapped toward Geraldo. "What?" she said, more sharply than she intended. "Didn't you hear me?"

"*Sí*, but—"

"Just do it," she said. "I don't mean to seem sharp, Geraldo. But untie him and let him get on his way." And then, after bidding good night to a puzzled MacGregor and Miguel, she reined her horse around, said, "All right, Jane, let's go," and started back through the darkness, back toward the ranch.

And, she hoped, back toward some understanding of the situation, which had gone from tangled to tied up in knots in the space of one night.

18

"You say they hired Grant Taylor?" Rance asked. "Your Maddie and her gals? They hired him? It wasn't somebody else?"

"You gettin' senile, Rance?" Slocum asked, grinning.

It was late afternoon, and they were about an hour's ride from the ranch. Over the last two days, Slocum had become more trusting of his old friend and they'd talked over a passel of things, including the weather, old times, how the government was going to hell, and Maddie's gold. But not this particular subject, which had just come up.

"That's about the third time you've asked me," Slocum said.

"Well, the first time or two was back in Vista Verde, and I was drunk," Rance said indignantly. "I was just askin' to be sure."

"Yes, Rance," said Slocum with exaggerated patience as well as a grin. "They hired Grant Taylor. Who, if I ain't mistaken, was the same feller I found in pieces on the desert. Don't know what killed him, though."

"You can be fair sure it was Loomis," the older

gunfighter said, setting his jaw. "Him, or one of his men. They're hell on wheels, and if they got hold of the news that the ladies had hired a gun, it'd be just like Loomis to swat him like a fly afore he got settled and started makin' trouble. Goddamn it!"

"What?" Slocum asked, surprised. "Why're you so shook over some hired-out shootist you don't even know?"

"I knew him, all right," was the answer. "Known him for years."

"Oh," Slocum said, and pulled his hat brim lower on his face. "I'm right sorry then, Rance. I didn't know you were acquainted."

"Damn straight, we was," Rance said, staring straight ahead. "That sonofabitch was mine to kill and nobody else's. Goddamn it anyway!"

"Huh?"

"Five years back," Rance said, "that weasel-assed Taylor lit out of Tucumcari on the best little sorrel filly this side of the Mississippi, and she just happened to belong to me. Nobody steals my horse, Slocum, nobody." He looked over, glaring. "I believe we had this conversation once time before."

Slocum swallowed. Once he'd hotfooted it out of Tombstone on a dandy dapple-gray gelding that just happened to be owned by Rance. He was going to Tucson for the Army—which he'd thought was a reasonable excuse—and he'd brought the grey back, but Rance had been madder than a wet hen, and had taken a couple of potshots at him.

It had taken a whole lot of apologizing and a whole lot more whiskey to get him calmed down, and it seemed he still hadn't wholly forgiven Slocum.

There was no quicker way to get on Rance's bad side than to mess with his horse.

Of course, Slocum held his mounts pretty dear too. He understood.

"You never caught up with him?" Slocum asked.

Rance leaned forward and spat down to the gravely desert. "Been trailin' him since, off an' on. Don't suppose you found a bloodred mare out there with him, did you?"

"Nope. Not red nor black nor pied. Not even so much as a scrap of saddle leather."

"Hmm."

"Y'know," Slocum said, "Grant Taylor probably sold that mare off years ago."

Rance shook his head. "Nope. Taylor would'a kept her, unless she got so stove-up he had to shoot her. She was too good a horse to sell."

Rance reached into his pocket and pulled out his silver cigar case, then held it out over the space between their horses, offering it to Slocum. Slocum never saw him replenish the stock, but it was always full. Not one to argue with divine providence, however, he accepted a cigar gladly, bit the end off, and spat.

Rance took one for himself, snipped the end, and lit it.

"If the coyotes ate Taylor like you say," Rance said, looking skyward, "they would'a made short work of a horse too. But there would'a been some sign, I'm thinkin'. I wonder if Loomis has got any new additions to his remuda."

Slocum paused, holding his lit sulfur-tip inches from his cigar. He cocked a brow. "You decide to ride on over there instead of stayin' with us?"

"Yeah, I reckon so," the red-haired gunman replied thoughtfully. "Who better to strut straight into the henhouse than a rooster?" Then he scowled. "And light that damn thing before you go and singe your fingers off! I swan, Slocum, you beat everything! You got bullet holes in your hat and a rip in your spare shirt. Slug tear through that too?"

Rance shook his head. "Last thing you need is to go burnin' your gun hand, seeing as how that's about all you got left that's in one piece."

Slocum rode into Maddie's alone, Rance having cut him loose and headed off toward the Loomis place well before Maddie's ranch house came into sight. He was half-afraid of what he'd find, given his past experience, but everything appeared just the way he'd left it, except for the absence of the flock.

"MacGregor has them down in the south flats," Maddie explained, after she'd practically kissed him silly right in the middle of the yard.

"Pedro," he said, "take my mare and—"

"Walk her out good and do the curry combing, and then the water, and then the oats," the squat Pedro said, taking Bess's reins. "I know. You see how many more adobe bricks we have made, Señor?"

Slocum looked, and then he blinked. Row upon row of new bricks had been set out to cure. Jane and Charity were down there, pulling molds off new blocks. Geraldo was throwing straw into the mud pit. Mace Cantrell, looking lovesick as usual, was working the straw into the mire, and his brother Mike was toting water. Over the scorched earth, someone had already pegged out the perimeter of the foundation for the new barn, and begun to dig the footings.

It was going to be a good barn, perhaps better than the old one. Certainly larger, and certainly less combustible.

"You boys work fast, Pedro," Slocum said. "That's a heap of blocks."

"We girls work fast too," Maddie said, tugging at his sleeve, urging him toward the ranch house. "Don't forget there's a female side to the labor force around here."

"Couldn't if I tried," he answered with a grin, and as Pedro led his mare off, he let Maddie pull him up onto the porch and inside.

"Got something to tell you," they both said at once.

Then, as one, they said, "You first."

Maddie started to laugh, and Slocum grinned. "You," he said.

Maddie wiped her eyes. "Don't know why I'm laughing. Lord knows, I can't find any humor in the situation. Christ, but it's good to have you back, Slocum."

He pulled out a chair and sat down, saying, "That's the impression I got when you practically threw me to the ground out front." She'd been making adobe bricks right alongside the others, but even through the mud spatters on her face and hands and the smears on her skirts, she still looked great.

Fortune or no fortune, she gave his chest a little shove, then sat down on his lap. "I'll throw you to the ground soon enough, cowboy," she whispered in his ear.

"If I give you the chance, darlin'," he said with a chuckle. "Let's hurry up and get the talkin' out of the way. Been thinking about you all the way from Vista Verde." He ran his hand up her side, and skimmed his fingers over the plump swell of her breast. The heat of her body rose through the fabric, tickling his fingertips.

"Course," he added thoughtfully, "we could talk any old time. I have all of a sudden got a powerful urge to take myself a bath."

Maddie, nibbling his earlobe, teased, "All by your lonesome, cowboy?"

Well, hell. Telling her about Rance wasn't all *that* urgent. He stood up, lifting her in his arms. He was almost surprised that he was already suddenly hard. "Maybe I could bypass that bath," he said, carrying her toward the hall.

She raked her teeth along his jaw, and ended at his ear, saying, "Good idea, Slocum. How *do* you come up with them?"

"Reckon they just rise up all on their own accord," he said, giving her bedroom door a kick. It swung in obediently, and he headed for the bed.

"Table," Maddie murmured.

He stopped. "You sure?"

"Table."

He carried her to the little table, just big enough for two people to sit at. Kicking the chairs out of the way, he sat her on its edge.

"Now what?" he said with a grin. As if he didn't know.

Her fingers went to the straining buttons of the front of his pants. "Seems to me you could have got back faster, Slocum," she said as one by one, she undid the buttons until she freed him, aching for action and fully aroused.

She held him in both hands, running her palms

up and down his length, then gave him a firm squeeze and let go. She lay back, pulling her skirts and petticoats up with her.

"Reckon you'd better rip my knickers off and go to it, darlin'," she said, her eyes half-lidded. "I've been missing you something fierce. Been thinking about you all day, and I'm just about ready to pop."

He was more than ready. "Anything for a lady," he said, and with one tearing motion, cleared a path for himself in the fabric.

Maddie closed her eyes, although it did nothing to veil the look of eager anticipation on her heart-shaped face. "Now," she said. "Now."

He studied her face—eyes lidded, lips trembling and slightly parted, a thin sheen of perspiration covering her brow—and he said, "Not quite yet, Maddie darlin'."

Before she could say, "What?" he reached down, took both her legs behind the knees, and raised them up. Settling her legs on his shoulders, he slowly ran his hands down her thighs to her buttocks and pulled her closer, until her fanny was half hanging off the table.

Through clenched teeth, she whispered, "Slocum, please!"

"Wait," he whispered, and skimmed one hand around her hips, then down, between her legs. She was already drenched in her own juices, and when he slid a finger within her, he found her interior wet and slippery, the muscles pulling and pushing at his finger.

"Slocum!" The command was weak, almost pleading. With one of her hands gripping the side of the table, the other stroked her own breast through the fabric of her bodice. "Slocum, now!"

He positioned himself at her threshold, letting the head rub up and down, but not entering, until Maddie's hand came free of the table's edge and, in frustration, started to smack down on the table-top repeatedly.

He pushed into her all at once, and her gasp at being entered changed immediately to the convulsions of orgasm. Slocum didn't stop, though. He kept riding her, pounding into her. Soon she'd locked her legs behind his neck and taken hold of the table again, and she was bracing against his every thrust, meeting it with a strange sort of savagery.

She came again, with a babbling shriek and a convulsion that nearly took her off the table and to the floor, but Slocum caught her. He tore at her bodice, ripped until the buttons popped, then tore at her camisole until her breasts were free. And then he began to twist one pink nipple, still thrusting into her, not breaking the rhythm.

Gently at first, then more firmly, he kept twisting it, teasing it, while Maddie, her eyes closed, her body gyrating as if it had been taken over by demons, chanted, "God! Yes, more! Please! Slocum!"

And at last he couldn't hold off any longer. He came into her so hard, with such power, that it felt for a moment as if his boots didn't touch the floor, as if he'd been thrown off a bronc and was sailing, just sailing, and he was never going to hit anything but cloud.

He opened his eyes with a start, because he didn't remember having closed them. And he found Maddie, still impaled on his cock, and shivering with the aftereffects of her third climax. Lazily, her hands rose from the table to her midsection, then her breasts.

Cradling one plump bosom in each hand and fairly purring, she looked up at Slocum. Slowly, she smiled. "Again?" she asked demurely.

Well, as demurely as possible for someone in her present position.

Chuckling, he slid out of her and pulled her skirts down. "Mind if I sit down for a minute first?" he asked, buttoning himself back up. He picked up the chairs he'd knocked over and righted them, then sat down with a thud.

Maddie slipped off the table, though she did nothing to close the front of her dress, and sat opposite him. He could still see the wet streaks on the wooden tabletop, the wet streaks of her juices and his semen.

She smiled at him. Her face was glowing.

"What?" he asked, weary from his exertion. "No applause?"

Grinning, she clapped her hands three times— one for each orgasm, he supposed—and then teased him, saying, "The least you could do would be to take your hat off."

He felt his face turn red, and Maddie began to laugh, her breasts jiggling with her chuckles. "Guess I wasn't the only one in such an all-fired toot, you old buzzard."

Sheepishly, Slocum took off his hat and sent her a lopsided grin. "Reckon you weren't." He paused.

"Maddie?"

She leaned forward, grinning. "Slocum?"

"Much as I hate to ask it, could you close up your dress? The scenery's awful pretty, but I've got to talk to you, and they're doin' a good job of distractin' me."

She laughed. "Good to know I'm not losing my charms. Tell you what," she said, rising. "I'll change, and then I'll fix you some dinner, and then we'll talk."

"No. I want to talk before everybody else comes in."

"All right, Slocum," she said, her brow furrowing slightly. She picked up a shawl and wrapped it around her. "Go ahead. I'm listening."

19

Maddie listened intently while Slocum recounted his meeting with Rance Peabody. She was enraged when Slocum told her that a friend of his had been hired by Loomis, and then relieved when he said that Rance appeared to be leaning toward their side. It still didn't set quite right with her, though.

"But you said he rode over to Loomis's?" she asked warily.

But Slocum seemed almost lackadaisical. "He said something about a rooster in a henhouse. Guess you'd say that Rance figured to be the rooster, and Loomis owns the henhouse."

"What?"

"Hell, Maddie," Slocum said with a shrug and a grin. "If he'd come back here with me, then you wouldn't have got to say hello nearly so nice as you just did."

Maddie shook her head slowly. "Ah, go on with ye, Slocum," she said, feigning an Irish lilt. "I'd've had a better greetin' for ye, if only ye hadn't cut me off mid-hello."

He laughed, and she was tempted to reach across the table for him again, such was its effect on her. She liked his laugh. She liked most everything about him.

But instead, she hugged the shawl about her more tightly, said a short, silent prayer, and asked, "And how'd you come out at the assayer's office?" For a question asked so lightly, it was of resounding importance.

"Maddie?" His expression suddenly deadly serious, he reached out and took her hands. She barely noticed her shawl falling loose again.

"What?" she said, fearing the worst. "It's fool's gold, isn't it?" She gripped his hands tighter. "Lord help us, we're poor again. I knew in my heart that we couldn't be so damn-fool lucky that we'd strike it rich twice. Well, I'm not going to work for Loomis, none of us are, and you can be sure of that! He's not going to win. I'll die before—"

"Maddie!" he said, wincing. "Maddie, ease up. You're about to squeeze my dang thumbs off."

"Sorry." She let go and put her hands to her face. "Tell me then."

"All I can tell you, Maddie, is that you'd better buy more land."

She looked up with a jerk. "Are you crazy?"

"You heard me. Buy more land." He grinned wide, and this time she could have slapped him just for being so ornery. "It's high grade, Maddie girl."

High grade. Something she hadn't dared to dream of.

"Now, I figure it's washing down from the Bradshaws," he went on. "There's probably a whole river of gold running down across your land in that dry streambed, if you want to dig for it." He grinned. "The source of it's higher up. Who owns that land?"

"N-nobody," she stuttered. It seemed she'd gone from being as poor as a church mouse to richer that Croesus in the space of half a minute, and frankly, it had left her numb. "Nobody," she repeated. "The government, I guess."

"Well, tomorrow you'd best take everybody off mudbrick detail and send 'em up to that canyon with a bunch of shovels and a couple of wagons," he said, grinning like a tomcat with a gullet full of Aunt Rhoda's canary. "Reckon you're back in business."

"And Loomis?" she said. "I don't think he's going to be as easy to convince."

Slocum patted his pocket. "That's taken care of. I've got to ride over and serve him with papers tomorrow, but it's all legal. He can't sue you for water rights that aren't his to begin with. Although," he said, leaning forward again, "if that had been his water you gals were using, you could have been in a peck of trouble."

"Why?" she asked, suddenly feeling rich enough to be arbitrary on a grand scale. She liked the feeling just fine. "What could he have done?"

"Moved you into that whorehouse of his, for starters."

His gaze slipped down her front, and she remembered the shawl. She hugged it about her again. "Pish," she said, dismissing the notion with a wave of her hand. "Just a bunch of balderdash! Loomis has got about as much sense as a newborn calf."

Slocum looked up and shook his head. " 'Fraid you're wrong, Maddie. This lawyer fella I talked to—this Mr. Foxworthy—tells me there's some old law on the books that says if you owe somebody a debt and can't pay it, then they can make you work it off any way they see fit. And in this particular case," he said, "you ladies would have worked it off on your backs."

Of all the dad-blamed nerve! She stood straight up, angrily announcing, "Slocum, that's indentured servitude!"

"I didn't make the law, Maddie," he said, holding up his hands as if to ward her off. "I'm just tellin' you about it."

"Slavery!"

"Maddie . . ."

"Of all the gall!" she shouted. "Of all the bark! And here I thought the stinking old polecat was just bluffing, when all the time he was actually going to do it!"

"Maddie, calm down."

She stalked to the window, then paced back again, wanting to hit something but not wanting it to be Slocum.

"Maddie, he can't do it now," Slocum soothed. "You're in the clear, darlin'."

She whipped round to face him. "You don't understand, Slocum. That slimy sonofabitch wasn't just threatening me with his whorehouse. He was threatening his own kin, that's how low he is!"

Slocum's face twisted. "You're his kin? Maddie, honey, that just doesn't make any—"

"No, you idiot," she snapped, then felt sorry for it. She closed her eyes, pressing the lids tight, then opened them. "Sorry. No, it's not me."

Slocum still didn't seem to understand, so she said, "Jane knew all along."

Slocum shook his head like a retriever shaking river water from its coat. "Back up," he said, confused. "You ain't makin' sense. What in tarnation did Jane know?"

Maddie sighed. She understood it—two nights ago, she'd practically had to pull the story out of Jane with a block and tackle—but explaining it was going to take some doing. Particularly since Slocum would want it quick and to the point, and not in a three-hour jumble, the way she'd gotten it from Jane.

She said, "Maybe . . . maybe I'd better start from the beginning?"

"Maybe you'd better," he said, "because starting from the middle ain't gettin' us nowhere."

Just then, a tentative voice came from the window. "Um, Señor Slocum? Señorita Maddie?"

Maddie and Slocum looked at each other, and then Slocum leaned forward and barked, "What?"

The unseen owner of the voice—who was Geraldo—said, "We are hungry. We are wanting to know if we can come in the house, or if you are . . . if you are using it."

Maddie covered her mouth with her hands and chuckled behind them as she watched Slocum turn beet red.

"Well, of course you can come in," he thundered. "What'd you think?"

"Just checking," came the muttered reply.

Slocum sat there a moment, and then looked at her. Consternation was all over his face. "What is it, Maddie? Do those knuckleheads think that we do it in every nook and cranny of the place every damn chance we get?"

Maddie couldn't help it. She started laughing again, and this time, it was out loud.

Slocum had the good sense to look even more embarrassed. "Aw, shit," he said. "That does it. Any immediate danger of Jane blowing up or pullin' a shotgun, somethin' like that?"

She shook her head. She was too busy laughing to say anything.

"Then I'm not gonna try to untangle this thing

on an empty stomach. Let's have some dinner.''
And then he looked her up and down, and with a
pained expression, added, ''And change that dress,
will you please? The sight of your tits is about to
drive me peach-orchard crazy.''

And before she realized that she'd been side-
tracked, and that she hadn't told him a thing, Slocum was out the door.

''Pass them biscuits, Miss Jane,'' Mace said. To
Slocum, the boy didn't look any less gooey-eyed
than when Slocum had left for Vista Verde several
days ago. If anything, he appeared more lovesick
than ever.

''Don't believe I ever had me such good biscuits,'' Mace gushed.

Jane growled at him and passed the basket of
biscuits, and then the butter, saying, ''I didn't
make them. Maddie did. She *always* makes the
biscuits. Although it's a miracle she could bake
anything, what with all the racket you made last
night keeping us up till all hours.''

Apparently, Mace had been serenading at Jane's
window again—well, caterwauling at it anyhow—
but he didn't comment on that. At least he showed
no new wounds. Maybe Jane was softening up!

''Oh,'' he said dreamily, holding the butter dish.
''Well, they's right good anyhow. Bet they
would'a been even better if you'd'a been bakin'.''

On Slocum's right, Maddie rolled her eyes, then

helped herself to another ear of corn. She had to ask Mace twice to pass the butter before he woke up and handed it to her. Then she began slathering her corn—nothing tiny or fragile about her appetite, which was one of the many things Slocum liked about her.

She announced, "Tomorrow, Slocum's going to serve some legal papers on Loomis that should settle his hash but good."

Both Mace and Mike were too intent on the females at the table to comment, but Geraldo looked up from his plate and grinned. "Really? I would like to go along, Slocum. To see the look on his face."

Slocum nodded. "Reckon that can be arranged. MacGregor and Miguel out with the sheep?"

Geraldo said, "Always."

Maddie concurred. "Can't even get them to come in for a meal, let alone a bath."

Jane lifted her head. "Mollycoddlers, that's what they are." She swallowed a mouthful of quail stew, then frowned. "You'd think those stupid sheep couldn't take a step without them. Although it suits me fine. Two less mouths to feed. They do all their own cooking. Guess what we serve up isn't good enough for them."

Mace nodded in agreement at her every word. "Yes, ma'am. That sure is right."

Jane closed her eyes and, through clenched teeth, said, "Goddamn it, Mace! If I just take off my top and let my tits hang out, will you shut the hell up?''

Maddie grabbed her before she could undo the first button, and made Mace trade chairs with Pablo. So much for softening up.

"I think that your Mr. MacGregor is nice, Slocum," Charity piped up, much to the chagrin of young Mike Cantrell, whose gaze was fairly glued to her face. He had it bad, all right. He'd barely noticed that little tiff between Jane and his brother.

With her fork, Charity daintily speared a bite of potato from her plate, then paused it in midair, the gravy dripping. "I think Mr. MacGregor talks just wonderful." The fork went in her mouth.

Poor Mike looked as though she'd just plunged it into his heart.

"Maddie," Slocum said, helping himself to the stew, "I think you better bring out some more gals from Chicago as fast as you can."

Chewing, she replied, "You read my mind."

Mike remained moony-eyed, Mace kept on babbling, Jane kept on threatening to strip, and Slocum kept silent at the little domestic dramas unfolding before him. He busied himself with eating. Maddie hadn't said another word about whatever this thing was with Jane, but it was probably more tales from the lovelorn.

It was just what he needed, he thought as he ladled yet more stew onto his plate. Where was it written that he had to be the father confessor, the arbitrator? Why couldn't they handle their own problems?

He had to admit, though, as he dug into his third helping, that Maddie was sure a damn fine cook. If she hadn't turned to whoring, she could have made a damn fine living in the restaurant business. He supposed the meals alone were worth the aggravation of dealing with all this lovesick horseshit.

The chatter continued all around him, and he found himself sinking into a very contented mood. Tomorrow he'd ride over to the Loomis place and settle the legal papers on him, and Loomis'd quit harassing Maddie. The sheep were somewhere out there in the dark, capably guarded by Taggart MacGregor and the tongueless Miguel, and come next spring, Maddie and the girls would be shearing the sheep (or whatever it was a person did with the woolly bastards) and birthing lots of little lamb chops.

In Rance, he had a friend in Loomis's camp, at least for the time being. If Loomis was going to try anything funny, he'd have forewarning.

And the girls had their gold, although no one had told Charity and Jane yet. He had little doubt but what Maddie could get it hauled out just fine. She'd done it before.

Of course, there was that niggling question at the back of his mind—who was Loomis's kinfolk anyhow, and why the hell should it matter to Maddie?—but it was pretty small potatoes, considering the other impending disasters he'd righted. It could probably be fixed by giving somebody a swift kick in the pants.

All in all, he thought smugly, he'd turned around an explosive situation, and got it well in hand in practically no time.

And tonight? Tonight there'd be Maddie again. He pushed his plate away, smiled, and sat back with a belch.

"Señorita Maddie?" Pablo asked meekly. "I am wondering. What is for the dessert?" It shook Slocum from his reverie, and echoed his thoughts. He licked his lips in anticipation of the announcement.

What he got, however, was a cry of, "Hello the house! Anybody home?"

He knew the voice.

20

The noise at the table stopped immediately, and it was then that Slocum heard horses' hooves outside, scuffling the dust in the yard. Rance had come, but he hadn't come alone. Dad-blast it anyway! Slocum cursed himself for having ever trusted the dandified gunslinger.

"Geraldo!" he hissed to the hand, who was already at the mantel, taking down the rifles and shotguns. "You and Mace take the front windows. Pablo in the hall. Mike at the back door. And don't shoot at nothin' unless I tell you."

Maddie started to say something, probably to protest at being left out, but he didn't have time to stop and fool with her. He pushed past and went to the front door. He opened it.

Rance most assuredly hadn't come alone. There were riders with him, at least a half dozen. Loomis too.

Slocum closed the door behind him and leaned against a porch post. "Evening, Mr. Loomis," he said, ignoring Rance in the thin hope that maybe, just maybe, he had some sort of plan, and wasn't going to bite the hand that had poured whiskey down his throat. "Just droppin' by to say howdy?"

From atop the jug-headed bay that Slocum had "borrowed" only a few days ago, Loomis thundered, "I've come to give you and them whores final warning, you Rebel sonofabitch. I got the law here with me, and—" He turned in the saddle, searching the darkness. "Where the hell is Ward Semple?"

"Uh, here, Mr. Loomis," came the quavering reply. A medicine-hat paint came forward, bearing a rider much less impressive than his horse: a thin, sickly-looking man with a pinched face. He wore a badge pinned to his blue plaid shirt, and it glinted softly in the moonlight. "H-here I am," he said reluctantly.

"Christ," muttered Loomis. "Get the rest of the way up here then. I want this to be official." He twisted back toward Slocum. "You tell them whores to get packed and get to town, or I'll pack for 'em, understand? This place has been stealin' my water for God knows how long, and I aim to get my just retribution. They been served with papers, all legal, and they ain't done a damn thing besides bring sheep. Sheep!"

He half-choked on the word, as if just the thought of sheep made him physically ill.

Slocum flicked a glance in Rance's direction, but the gunman simply sat his horse, staring blankly toward the house.

"By God, Loomis!" Slocum said. He reached into his pocket and pulled out his fixings. He figured that as long as he played the situation casual, Loomis would keep his head. "I don't believe I've ever met a fella what could get himself in so much of an uproar over what amounts to diddly-squat. Because it appears to me," he went on, sprinkling fixings into the paper, "that you just rode all the way over here for nothin'. Well, not *exactly* nothin'." He gave the quirlie a lick and stuck it in his mouth.

"Nothin'? Slocum, you sonofabitch, don't you try to fancy-talk me!" Loomis's face was beginning to turn red. Casual didn't appear to be working.

But Slocum shrugged, and lit his quirlie anyway. "Fancy-talk? Why, Mr. Loomis, that's something I save for the ladies." He shook out the lucifer. "Wouldn't waste it on you."

This only made Loomis madder. "You ain't got that foreign sheep man and his trick killer dogs here to help you out tonight, no, sir! In fact," he said, pulling himself erect in the saddle, "I don't believe we'll wait till tomorrow at all. I believe I'll get this eviction under way tonight! Sheriff, do your duty!"

Sheriff Semple looked stricken. Obviously Loomis's man, and a weak one at that, he hadn't figured on anything like this. Once upon a time, he'd probably thought that once he was elected, he'd just sit in his office with his feet propped on the desk. That in such a quiet little burg as Three Wives, all he'd have to do would be to drink his coffee and collect his pay until the next election.

"I, uh . . ." he stuttered. "I, uh . . ."

"Goddamn it!" Loomis shouted. He tried a different tack. "Rance! Rance Peabody!"

Rance, who'd been sitting his horse quietly at the edge of the group of riders, eased his mount over to stand beside Loomis's.

"Hell's bells, Loomis! You don't have to go shoutin' all over the place," Rance drawled, straight-faced, and Slocum knew, then and there, that Rance was on his side. "I can hear you just fine. Hell, I'll bet they can hear you back at your place."

"Get these people out of this house!" Loomis commanded. "Get 'em off my land! And get rid of this . . . this . . . saddle tramp!"

"Saddle tramp?" Rance said lazily. "I think you're stretching it a mite. Why, I'd call John Slocum a whole mess of things—a sonofabitchin' bastard and backwoods Georgia cracker and the second-best shootist north of Sonora for starters—but saddle tramp wouldn't be one of them. 'Less, of course, we was just joshin' around. So tell me. You joshin', Mr. Loomis?"

And then suddenly, Slocum saw a too-familiar movement from one of the riders. In the same second that his hand went to his gun, he saw Rance pull iron too. That confused him a mite, and before he could decide who the hell to shoot at, two shots, one right on top of the other, had split the night, and there was a terrible, knifing pain in his left shoulder.

Just as he realized he'd been shot, just as rifle barrels hurriedly poked from the windows on either side of his back, he saw Loomis's rider topple from his horse. The man fell forward, and the lights from the house reached just far enough that he could see the man's face.

It was Ed Barlow.

"Hold your fire!" Slocum called. Loomis, who was just going for his pistol, wisely thought better of it.

At the same time Slocum heard Barlow give out a groan, the door behind him swung open with a creak. Suddenly, Maddie was beside him, a rifle at her shoulder, before the screen door could bang shut again. His gun, which he'd swung to cover Rance, just in case, moved to cover Barlow's writhing shape.

From the corner of his eye, he saw Rance roll his eyes as he reholstered his pistol. Despite the fire in his shoulder, Slocum allowed himself a small smile. Dang him anyway for ever doubting Rance for even a quarter of a second. He'd have to have words with him, though, about that "second-best shootist" crap.

Maddie didn't see his smile, though—and apparently, she hadn't seen what happened before it, or who had fired. She cried, "Loomis, you crazy bastard!" and swung the Winchester toward him.

Wincing with the pain, Slocum raised his left arm and pushed aside the barrel of her Winchester. It discharged, but the bullet went high and wide.

"Everybody, just hold your horses," he said through gritted teeth.

Belatedly, the sheriff said, "Uh, calm down now. Let's just take 'er easy, folks. Don't want no bloodshed here."

Slocum glowered. "A little late for that, don't you think, Semple?" And then, to Loomis, he said, "If you idiots'll give me half a minute before you set into blastin' again, I reckon I can take care of this thing."

He tried to go for his shirt pocket, but he couldn't do that and hold the gun on Barlow at the same time—at least, not with his good arm—so he told Maddie to cover Barlow, reholstered his Colt, and eased the papers from his pocket.

"I believe this oughta settle your hash, Loomis," he said, and walked out into the throng to hand the papers up to Sheriff Semple. Semple squinted at them to no avail before he flicked a lucifer into life and began reading.

While Semple was perusing the legal papers, Slocum said, "I got duly sworn in by the courts to deliver that, Sheriff." His arm burned as if somebody was holding a branding iron to it, and he held it close. He fought off the urge to walk over to Barlow's downed and groaning form and kick him square in the head.

Instead, he turned toward Loomis. "And you got no grounds, legal or otherwise, to go round evicting anybody. That's not your damn water they've been usin', not one single drop. This place was surveyed about ten years back, and that surveyor's map shows an underground river runnin' through this property, if a body knows how to look for the signs of it. An underground river that doesn't have squat to do with the Blue Calf."

"Bullshit!" said Loomis, the veins in his neck bulging. "Horse and goat and dog shit! Underground river, my horse's butt! I never heard of such a thing!"

"Beggin' you pardon, Loomis," Slocum said, nearing exasperation, "but it seems to me you couldn't't've lived in the southwest—let alone the Arizona Territory—for too long *without* hearin' of 'em. It's a common thing for water to go underground around here. Hell, look at the Santa Cruz, down Tucson way!"

Loomis wasn't hearing any of it. "I'll take this to a higher court, by Christ!" he fumed. "I'll have so many lawyers on these gals that—"

"Fine," said Slocum, cutting him off. "You just do that. Reckon these ladies'll have plenty of grounds for a counter-suit. They might even end up ownin' your spread before they're finished with it.''

Sheriff Semple, who had finished reading, handed the papers across to Loomis and shrugged. "Sorry, Mr. Loomis," he said, "looks legal to me." He backed his mount well away.

Loomis opened his mouth a time or two, but said nothing. And then, quite suddenly, he barked, "Get Barlow on his horse."

"Don't reckon that's such a good idea," said Rance. Slocum had almost forgotten about him. As he watched, Rance wove his horse through the throng to its middle, and snagged the reins of Barlow's mount, then led it clear. It was a sorrel mare, tall and bright bloodred, even breedier-looking than the liver-chestnut gelding Rance was presently mounted on. Slocum figured it'd be a sure bet that this was the mare that Grant Taylor had made off with all those years ago.

"Oh. And by the way, Mr. Loomis?" Rance added, straight-faced, "I quit."

Slocum held back his grin, and said, "Sheriff, I found a body a few miles west of here when I was ridin' in. It was the last remains of one Mr. Grant Taylor, gunfighter by trade. If you're of a mind, I can take you to his grave, seein' as how I dug it. It's my guess that your friend Ed Barlow there had quite a bit to do with his being deceased. Rance can fill you in on where Barlow got that horse if you want to come round tomorrow." Over his shoulder, he shouted, "Geraldo!"

When the ranch hand appeared, a shotgun in his grip, Slocum relieved him of it and said, "Toss Barlow up behind the sheriff's saddle, would you?"

And then he noticed that Jane was peeking out through the window, and there was a very curious expression on her face. Fear? No, terror. So far as he knew, Jane wasn't afraid of anything, man nor beast, and her expression shook him.

He followed the line of her gaze to Loomis, who was staring right back at her. It didn't look like a gaze of admiration either.

A half second later, though, Loomis broke it off, and reined his horse around, saying, "You ain't heard the last of me, Slocum."

"Figured you'd say somethin' like that," Slocum replied wearily. He stood his ground until the last glimpse of the rumps of Loomis's men's horses—with the notable exceptions of Rance's two—had vanished into the night, and then, all at once, Slocum slumped to the ground.

"You're hurt!" Maddie cried, rushing to his side, as if she'd been too busy thinking about killing somebody to notice before.

"Aw, hell's bells," commented Rance, who was still mounted. He leaned forward on his saddlehorn. "He's barely scratched. Seen him take three or four like that of an evenin' and go out to kill twenty Injuns the next day.'' Just then, he must have seen Jane, who was still peering out the window, and tipped his hat. ''Evening, ma'am,'' he added.

Jane slammed the shutter.

By this time, Maddie and Geraldo had Slocum up on his feet and were half-carrying him toward the porch. ''I can walk, goddamn it,'' he grumbled, and shook them off.

''Fine,'' Maddie snapped at him, but her face was full of worry.

He took the steps, and nearly ran square into Mace, who was just coming out. His rifle was pointed at Rance. ''What you want I should do with this one?'' he asked.

Slocum sighed. Didn't anybody pay attention around here? ''Put up his horses and fix him some dinner, I reckon.''

''But—''

''Just do it, Mace,'' he said wearily, then added, ''Everybody, this here's Rance Peabody. Rance, this is everybody. Well, most everybody. I swear, seems to me that we got half the population of the Territory stayin' out here with us. Maddie?''

She came round in front of him, still looking worried, but still a little ticked off too. ''What is it, Slocum?''

''Honey, I reckon I maybe could use a little . . . a little . . .''

The world went black.

21

"There," said Maddie as she finished tying off his bandage. "That ought to take care of it." She stood up, taking the extra rags and the bowl of bloody water with her. She crossed the bedroom, golden with lamplight, and put them on the table.

"A fine thing, Slocum," she said, crossing her arms and regarding him archly. "A great big grown man, passing out on me like that. It only grazed you, for heaven's sake."

Slocum felt a blush rising up his neck. "Musta been because I just ate so much," he said. And when she lifted an eyebrow, he added, "Well, all my recuperative powers were busy digestin', Maddie! Besides, I didn't really pass out. Not *cold*."

She came, sat on the edge of the bed, and patted his hand. "Sure, honey," she said with a thinly disguised smirk.

He pushed himself up to lean against the headboard and sighed. "How long was I out? Not that I'm admittin' anything, mind."

She laughed. "Only about fifteen minutes, you big fake."

"Well," he grumbled, suddenly noticing he'd

been stripped of his shirt, "seems it was enough time for you to shuck me outta my clothes." He sat forward. "I'd better ride out and check on MacGregor and Miguel and those woolly rats of yours. No telling what—"

She pushed him back against the pillows. "Hush," she said. "Pablo and the Cantrell boys rode out about five minutes ago, loaded for bear. Although I doubt they're going to find any. Loomis sort of took off with his tail tucked between his legs."

"And Rance?"

"He's sitting out front at the table, inhaling some dinner. Probably eating your dessert by this time. Chocolate layer cake, in case you were wondering." She smiled. "I swan, Slocum. Some of the people you know!"

"Chocolate layer cake?" In the excitement, he'd forgotten all about dessert. "Maddie, did I say anything to Loomis about the gold?"

"Not that I heard."

"Damn. I wanted to shake him up with that one. Wanted to see the look on his face."

Maddie smiled and tousled his hair. "Well, you were more than a little busy out there. By the way, thank you for stopping me from putting a bullet through Loomis's thick skull."

"Having second thoughts?"

"No." She smoothed the coverlet. "But it would have been colossally stupid of me to do it right in front of Sheriff Semple, even if he is a dolt.''

Slocum nodded. ''True. Maddie?''

''Mm?''

''Maybe this'd be a good time for you to tell me about Jane.''

She folded her hands and stared at them. ''Good a time as any, I suppose. Where do you want me to start?''

Part of him wanted her to begin with that look he'd seen pass between Jane and Loomis out front a few minutes ago, but he said, ''The beginning's as good a place as any.''

Maddie sighed. She looked up. ''All right. It's a pretty long story, though. I'll try to make it short.''

''I'm all for that,'' he said with a nod.

''It involves Charity too. She comes from farm people, down in Missouri,'' Maddie began. ''Her family got burnt out when she was just a little thing. The bank took the land and everything they owned, and I guess they were practically begging on the roads inside a year.

''Charity got passed from one family to the next, and the next, and the next, until she was just coming sixteen and . . .'' She shook her head. ''Well, you've seen her, Slocum. Prettier than a just-opened daisy on a May morning. Fresh and vulnerable. Which was just the thing to tempt Felicity—that's the woman who ran the house where we all worked.''

"Felicity. I know. When are we gonna get to the part where Jane comes into this?" Slocum asked. "Not to mention Loomis."

Maddie gave his hurt arm a little thump, and he grimaced. "I said I'd give you the short version," she said curtly, "and I am. My Lord, Slocum, I just covered sixteen years in less than a minute! Can I go on now?"

Still stinging, Slocum nodded. "Just don't go love-pattin' that arm again, okay?"

Maddie's brow furrowed. "Oh! Oh, I didn't realize! Sorry, honey."

"It's all right," he lied. "The story?"

"All right. Where was I? Oh, Charity had come to work with us at Felicity's. The next part is Jane. All right?"

He nodded.

"Jane was working at Felicity's too. In fact, Jane—and Ann-Elizabeth, the other girl I brought out—was there before I was. Jane used to handle most of the rougher trade. You know, the men who wanted somebody to really whip them or to—"

As interested as he might have been in the sexual peccadillos of the rich, he cut her off. "Maddie?" he said gently.

"Sorry. Anyway, Jane sort of took Charity under her wing. Well, we all did, but Jane especially. I was already in Arizona by the time it happened, though." She paused to stare out the window, as if thinking.

Slocum said, "By the time what happened?"

Her head jerked back. "By the time that Loomis came into our house," she said, "by the time that Jane heard him, out in the hallway, saying that—"

"What the hell was Loomis doing in Chicago?"

"Came up with a herd of his cattle, I suppose," she said rather abruptly. "Chicago's getting to be the world's stockyard, isn't it? And stop interrupting me. Anyway, he was talking with his friend, pointing at Charity—and all excited—and whispering that he'd bet anything that gal was none other than his sister's girl, the sister who'd married a farmer and come to no good. Said she was a dead ringer for her mama."

She had Slocum's attention now. He waited for her to go on.

Maddie's lips tightened. "He said, seeing as how she was spoiled already, that maybe he'd pull her out of the parlor that night and take her upstairs. He said it couldn't hurt anything, what with her being her being a whore already, and ruined. And then he said, 'By God, ain't she just Francine's double!'

"Right up till that moment, Jane thought he was just blowing smoke. You know, like men'll do when they come into an establishment like that. But at that very second, when he said his sister's name was Francine, Jane knew he was telling the truth.

"Jane could have bent a candlestick over his head right then and there—and I suppose she wanted to in the worst way—but she went to find Felicity, more's the pity. When Felicity talked to him—didn't mention anything that Jane had heard, of course—and found out what his tastes were, she paired him up with Jane for the evening."

Maddie shook her head. "And Jane? She didn't know what to do. I guess we girls had more respect for Felicity than sense, though, because Jane finally decided to just go do her job. I guess she figured she didn't want to cause trouble for Felicity, and anyway, the time Loomis spent with her was time he couldn't spend with Charity.

"So she led him to her room. Where, to make a long story short, he didn't want to play nice, and he got the upper hand. He gagged Jane and tied her to a chair, and beat her near-senseless before he had his way with her. In every possible way, if you get my meaning."

Slocum found himself shaking with rage. "The bastard," he said through clenched teeth. "The sorry sonofabitch. I should've killed him when I had the chance, when he was sittin' out there on his horse like he was the goddamned King or somethin'."

Maddie put a hand on his chest. "I haven't got to the meat of it yet, Slocum."

He heard a small sound at the door to the hall,

and looked up to see Jane standing there, her face drained of blood.

"I see you can't keep anything to yourself, Maddie," Jane said flatly. "I should've known better than to trust you."

"Jane—" Maddie began.

Slocum cut her off. "You'd better come the rest of the way in, Jane," he said. He didn't have any idea how long she'd been standing there, but it appeared to have been long enough that she knew Maddie had aired her dirty linen.

Jane hesitated, and Maddie started to get up, but Slocum gripped Maddie's arm and pulled her back.

"C'mon, Jane," he coaxed. Maybe he'd get the story firsthand. He just hoped it would be without Jane getting mad and flinging something. Considering all the quilts Maddie'd had him swathed in— and for just a little scratch on his arm!—he wasn't in any position to move quick.

When she hesitated, he said, "Jane, I know it's hard, and I guess I can see the reasons you've got for dislikin' the male sex so much. But you gotta have a little faith. I ain't here to hurt you."

More softly, he added, "I won't lie to you— I've done plenty'a bad things in my day—they weren't none of 'em to women, but they were bad things all the same. And I've had worse things done to me. But I want to help you ladies. And I can't unless you come clean with me."

As he spoke, Jane's face had gradually softened.

"All right," she said in a small voice. She came and sat in one of the chairs at the table, across the room from Maddie and Slocum. She steepled her fingers and stared at her nails for a moment, then looked up, all hard edges again, and said, "But get this, Slocum. If you're lying to me, or if any harm comes to Charity, so help me God, there won't be any safe place for you on this green earth."

If anybody had ever meant anything, Jane did. Slocum judged that she intended to chase him down and gut him like a carp if he failed her. He had a queasy feeling that she could do it too.

He said, "I swear to you, I'll do my best."

Maddie added, "He's a good man, Jane." She smiled. "Not worth a tinker's damn for sticking around for the everyday parts, mind, but he always turns up when things get rough."

"Gee, thanks," he mumbled.

"I heard what Maddie said," Jane started. "About Chicago, that is. It was pretty much right, and you don't need any more details."

Slocum nodded.

Jane looked at him for a moment, as if to make certain she had quashed any prurient interest on his part, then continued. "Later on, after Loomis left and the doc got done with me, I was still panicked about Charity. About him being her niece, and about him wanting to . . . well, you know. I guess I pitched a fit with Felicity, on account of she seemed a little lackadaisical about the whole thing. But she promised to boot him off the premises, should he ever show up again looking for entertainment.''

''Did he?'' Slocum asked. He didn't want to think about that ''fit'' she'd thrown with her ex-employer. Jane being Jane, it was a wonder the whorehouse walls were still standing.

Jane shook her head. ''No, he didn't. And to tell the truth, I sort of forgot about him. Shoved him right out of my mind, he was that distasteful. That is, till Maddie here sent for us.''

''We all went into town one day, Jane and Charity and Ann-Elizabeth and me,'' Maddie said, ''and Loomis was coming out of the bank—''

''Where else?'' Jane cut in, sarcastically.

''—and we nearly ran into him,'' Maddie continued.

''That's right,'' Jane said, the familiar venom creeping into her voice.

''I thought it was strange at the time,'' Maddie said. ''The way he looked at us—at Jane and Charity in particular. Like he was putting together the pieces of a puzzle.''

Jane's face was set. ''The bastard tipped his hat to Charity and Ann-Elizabeth and Maddie, and when he walked past me, all he said was, 'Got fond memories of you, whore.' He said it real low so that the others didn't hear, only me, and I didn't let on that I'd heard him. And then we didn't see him for a real long time.''

"We heard when he started putting up that damn whorehouse," Maddie interjected.

"And this was right after Loomis found the nugget, the one that Mike told Maddie about?" Slocum asked, hoping to urge her on.

"What nugget?" said Jane, one eyebrow lifted.

Maddie said, "I'll tell you later," then turned back to Slocum. "Yes, it was," she said. "And a couple months after Ann-Elizabeth took off for who-knows-where."

"It was about then that he sent Ed Barlow to call on me for the first time," Jane said, taking over again. "Barlow said that Loomis had done his research, that we'd been swiping his water, and that he could have us kicked off our land—Maddie's land—just by pulling a few strings. He said that Loomis was fed up with us trying to bring in sheep, and that he wouldn't have any more of it, and that he was building a nice shiny new whorehouse in town and that he was going to put us in it.

"Barlow just said that either I helped Loomis get Maddie to move off the land—to sell out or abandon it—or else Loomis was going to make good on his threat. I got the distinct impression from Barlow that Loomis could do it too. And Barlow said he was going to be seeing me on a regular basis, if I got his drift, and Loomis was going to take up a lot of Charity's time.''

She paused, and Slocum thought she was on the verge of tears: not the sweet, helpless kind—the kind that made a fellow want to go and put his arm around a gal and comfort her—but angry, acid tears.

She didn't cry, though, although her eyes glistened with moisture. Instead, she said, "I got this idea in my head that I could handle it. That I could deal with it, and not let on a thing to Maddie or Charity. I figured to do what Barlow told me, just for a while, because sooner or later Loomis would have to rear his ugly head when there was nobody else around, and then I could kill the sonofabitch. Our troubles would be over. It's just . . .''

She paused, searching for the right words. "It's just that Loomis never showed himself, and the whole thing got out of hand. Just a little at a time, it slipped away from me.''

Slocum sighed. "I'll say. Jane, what on earth made you think you could kill him?''

She lifted her head haughtily. "I shot your hat off, didn't I?''

"I knew it!'' he said, sitting forward all of a sudden, and filled with righteous indignation. "Goddamn it Jane! You shot me in the damn sleeve too, didn't you?''

"Shot you in the sleeve?'' Maddie muttered softly, and giggled.

"Shot me in the goddamned sleeve of my

second-best shirt!'' he said in exasperation.

"It just sounds funny put that way, that's all,"
Maddie said, and even though she gave the appearance of trying to hold her mouth straight, she
didn't seem to be having too much luck. "Shot
you in the sleeve!"

"She could've killed me!"

Maddie doubled over, and then she couldn't
stop laughing. Slocum just looked at her, his
mouth hanging open. What was so funny about his
shirt? Why, that slug could have just as easily
taken his head off. And besides, he'd bought it in
Abilene, tailor-made, and it had cost him four dollars and change!

Jane scowled at the both of them, and said,
"Are you about done, Maddie?"

Maddie wiped at her eyes and said, between
snorts, "Oh, Jane. I'm sorry. It's just that everything's been so tense around here. Slocum's sleeve
just hit me funny, that was all." One last giggle
escaped her. "Sorry. Go on."

"Barlow . . . Maddie, stop it!"

"Sorry, Jane," Maddie said, and wiped the last
trace of a grin from her face. It helped that Slocum
pinched her. At least, she swatted at him, so he
supposed it did.

"All right. Barlow set the barn on fire, on
Loomis's orders," Jane continued warily. "Before
that, the first flock, the one that was butchered before it could get this far? That was all Loomis's

men's doing. Then he got me under his thumb, and I pulled a few strings—sent a few wires—and sold off the next flock of Maddie's sheep before they got anywhere near here.

"But the last flock?" she added with a shrug. "This one happened too fast. Maddie'd sent for the sheep and didn't tell anybody until the last minute, and then you showed up, Slocum, and helped bring them in.

"And before that, Barlow killed Maddie's gun-slinger." She flicked a glance at Slocum. "I guess you already knew that."

Actually, he hadn't—not until that very evening, when Rance had retrieved his stolen horse—but he nodded at her. He was thinking that with Jane shooting up his second-best shirt a few days ago and Barlow winging his third-best tonight, he was down to his last—and best—shirt. He'd be damned if he'd let somebody else ruin that one!

Jane stood up. "I guess you're thinking that this is all my fault," she said defiantly. "I guess you're thinking that if I'd told Maddie right off, may-be this whole thing could have been avoided. At least, that's what Maddie said to me when she found out the other night."

"Jane," Maddie said sternly, "don't put words in my mouth."

"It's what you meant," Jane said. "And maybe you're right. But I only did it to protect Charity, to keep her from having to go through what I did that night. Those things Loomis did to me," she added with a shudder so violent that she closed her eyes and wrapped her arms about her shoulders.

After a moment, she looked up again, and her eyes were filled with resolve. "To keep her—to keep all of us—from ever having to sell ourselves again."

Slocum started to say something, but she headed him off.

"You're gonna say that Charity and me could've just lit out, aren't you, Slocum? That's your answer to everything. You're going to say that we didn't have to stay with Maddie, and I suppose you're right. After all, Ann-Elizabeth up and took off, and took a damn buckboard with her! But we would have stayed, or at least, Charity would. She's that kind of girl, you know? And I would've stayed with her."

"You'd have stayed anyway, Jane," Maddie said softly.

Jane looked away. "Maybe," she muttered.

"Well, now you don't have to worry about that anymore," Slocum said. He swung his legs over the edge of the bed. Damn women anyway, putting him to bed when he was only scratched. "All water under the bridge. Loomis was after Maddie's gold."

Jane opened her mouth, but Slocum said, "Maddie'll explain later. I doubt that he gives a donkey's behind whether or not you're running woollies on this land," he went on. "And as for that whorehouse of his, that was just in case you gals were stupid enough to let that trumped-up water claim of his stand. Frosting on the cake, as far as he was concerned."

He grabbed his boots and tugged the first one on. "He was bound and determined to pry you off this place by any means possible. But now that we've got the legalities behind us—and that fancy lawyer in Vista Verde says those maps are clear enough to hold up in any court of law—he can't throw you off your land. He can't work you any way he sees fit for stealing his water. Stupid bastard." He tugged on the second boot. At least Maddie'd left his britches on. For a change.

"Jane," he said, "I think you've been makin' yourself crazy for no reason."

"No," she said. "A very good reason. Charity still doesn't know anything about that scum being her kin. And I'll thank you to keep it that way."

The look she gave him was filled to the brim with unspoken threats—and a simple plea.

He said, "She won't hear it from me, Jane. And I reckon you ladies have seen the last of Loomis." Then, craning his head around the room, he added, "Where's my shirt?"

Maddie said, "It's in the mending bag. Why don't you—"

He held up a hand, silencing her. Shots, and lots

of them, were coming from far away.

Jane's face screwed up. "Is somebody outside making popcorn?"

"Rance!" Slocum shouted, striding to the door while Maddie went for the mending bag and his bloody shirt. By the time he reached the front room and was halfway into his sleeves, Rance was already on his feet and out on the porch, his layer cake left half-eaten on the table.

"They's a good ways out, Slocum," he called as Slocum, followed by Maddie, joined him. He was pointing to the southwest. "Over thataway. Where'd you say them boys had your sheep, Miss Maddie?"

Slocum answered for her. Doing up his buttons, he said, "They move 'em all the time." Then he added, "Sparse grazing," by way of explanation.

Kate handed him his hat and his gunbelt. "Where's Geraldo?" he asked as he hurriedly strapped the guns on and settled the hat on his head.

"I sent him north," Maddie said quickly. "It was his watch."

They were all moving quickly toward the corral by then. Charity had joined them, and her questions of "What is it?" and "What's going on?" and "Is that somebody shooting?" were bouncing off Slocum like tiny hailstones.

He didn't answer her. Nobody did. As Jane bundled her back to the house and Maddie hung on the corral fence and he and Rance saddled their horses, all he could think about was Loomis.

And all he could think about him was, *That goddamn idiot!*

22

Slocum and Rance crept on hands and knees through the brittle weeds to the top of a small rise, and peered down at the campfire. The flock was scattered, and worse. Slocum could see two dead ewes at the edge of the firelight, blood soaking their fleeces.

Closer to the fire was the thing he didn't want to see—Miguel's brightly dressed body was sprawled and lifeless, one booted foot smoking in the fire. In one hand, he clutched a rifle. The other rested on the corpse of a black and white sheepdog.

No, not a corpse. The dog lifted its head and whined softly. Slocum could have sworn it looked right at him.

MacGregor, as well as the rest of the sheep and Loomis's men, were nowhere to be seen. Maddie's men weren't around either.

Beside him, Rance said what Slocum was thinking. "Hell's bells! Why couldn't Loomis do his shootin' in broad daylight like a regular rowdy? Gonna be sinful hard to track 'em if they've gone any distance."

Slocum slithered back down the slope, and Rance followed. Both men climbed on their horses. "Not gonna follow 'em," Slocum said coldly, reining his horse around. "Gonna check on that dog and pull poor Miguel outta the fire, and then I'm goin' to ride over to Loomis's ranch and wait for him. Maybe give him a little surprise greetin'."

"What about your sheep man?"

"He can take care of himself," Slocum replied. He hoped it was true, and that MacGregor wasn't lying dead in some ravine.

In the end, they took the dog with them. It wasn't hurt bad enough to put out of its misery, but it was too hurt to leave for the coyotes. After he and Rance hauled Miguel's body up the closest tree to keep it safe from predators, he did a little quick bandaging on the dog, and slung her up gently behind Rance's saddle.

"Gonna have to do," he said, mounting Bess again. "Can you keep it steady?"

"The damn dog or the damn horse?" Rance asked in disgust as his chestnut skittered under him. "Thought I was gonna be roundin' up that crew of Loomis's, not nursemaidin' no sheepdog."

Slocum sighed. "Shut up and lead the way, will you?"

• • •

Loomis's spread—the Lazy L, according to the signs, and the brands, which seemed to have been burned into everything in sight—was a sprawling adobe ranch. By the looks of it, nobody was home yet, but Slocum and Rance—after depositing the dog in a safe place near the corral—made a check of the barn and bunkhouse and the outbuildings. They were devoid of human life.

After peeking in the windows, Slocum determined that the only person in the house itself was a Chinese cook. Slocum took the front, Rance took the back, and they crept toward the middle. When they burst in on him, the cook was so startled that he threw the bowl of beans he was snapping straight up into the air, and the bowl hit him on the head, knocking him senseless.

"Well, that's a new one on me," Rance said, scratching his temple.

"Tie him up and toss him in a bedroom or something," Slocum growled.

His arm was hurting him worse than it should, and he was secretly worried about MacGregor. He figured that Loomis was bound to come galloping in with half-a-dozen men at any moment, and frankly, he didn't yet have much of a plan as to what he was going to do once Loomis got there.

"Tie him up, Rance," Rance grumbled. "Haul the dog, Rance. Don't finish your cake, Rance."

"Rance?"

"What?"

"Shut up."

"Hmph," Rance snorted, and dragged the unconscious cook down the hall toward the bedroom doors.

Slocum started back up toward the parlor. It was the house of a rich man, all right: leather furnishings—their wooden arms stamped with the Lazy L brand—a large stone fireplace crowned by whitetail racks and the headgear of a longhorn steer, and two shelves of floor-to-ceiling books and china knickknacks.

He wondered if he should greet Loomis here, or let him get settled first, then step out of the darkness.

There was a sudden crash and thud, and then Rance whispered, "Slocum?"

Slocum had drawn his gun and dropped to his knees at the sound. Letting out his breath, he turned toward Rance's voice. "What?" he hissed.

"I, um, I think you better come see this for yourself."

Giving a last glance out the window and muttering, "Shit," he stood and turned on his heel. "What's so all-fired important?"

Rance popped out of a doorway, and motioned to him. "C'mere."

Slocum followed, and stepped into a pitch-black room. Rance grabbed his arm, keeping him from entering further. "Careful you don't trip over the Chink," he said.

There was the sound of a lucifer scratching into life, and then a burst of light. Slocum blinked once, then blinked again. A strange, stale odor came to his nostrils. It was faint, but it was there.

"Ain't it the damnedest thing you ever seen?" Rance said. "I drug the Chinaman in here, thinkin' it was a bedroom. Sure ain't no bedroom, though. You think he butchers steers in here or somethin'?"

"Light a lamp," Slocum said flatly. When the windowless room was illuminated, he turned slowly, studying the contents and the furnishings, then looked back at the door.

"You smash this lock, Rance?"

His friend shrugged. "I sorta fell against it when I was carryin' the Chinaman."

Slocum said, "Must've fallen hard. You took the damned thing clear off the hasp."

"Stop fooling around with the hardware, Slocum," Rance said. "Get a gander'a this place! Hell's bells! What's a fella use a room like this for anyways?"

Well, Rance wasn't quite as worldly as the impression he liked to give, and in that moment, Slocum liked him even more. Nobody should have to know about things like this or rooms like this. Particularly, what happened in them to the women they were intended for.

Ropes and leather straps, speckled with dried blood, dangled from the ceiling in the center of the room. Each came down to shoulder height or higher, and ended with a locking cuff. There were two benches—both with buckles and straps and moveable parts, and each spattered with dried blood—at the far end of the room. The walls were hung with an assortment of whips, from buggy whips to riding crops to short, multi-lashed whips with a lead sinker affixed to the end of each lash.

There were things that would leave gouges and bruises, things that could tear flesh or slice it, things with tiny, wicked hooks, things with blades. Things that would only be possessed by a man whose primary pleasure was to inflict pain.

Slocum had seen such things before, one time and one time only: when he was in a Chinese brothel up in Frisco. It had sickened him then, and it sickened him now.

A camera was set on its tripod in the middle of the room, aimed at the ropes and leathers. Focused right at the point where a person would be standing—if she were chained to the straps dangling from the ceiling—it was ready to snap a picture for posterity.

Loomis was one sick sonofabitch, all right. Sicker than anyone had imagined.

"Slocum?" Rance said again, and this time his voice was a little thick, a little choked. "What the hell is this place?"

He didn't answer. Slowly, as if his boots were deep in treacle, he walked to the far wall. There, between the dangling buggy whips and leather gags, the miniature branding irons and bamboo switches, a space had been cleared on the wall.

Pictures were thumbtacked to it. Not many, but enough. Enough to tell him that Loomis had been playing his little games for far too long. Slowly, Slocum pulled one photograph free and held it in shaking fingers. An Indian woman, naked and bleeding, was suspended by the leather straps. Her face was so distorted by contusions that she was barely recognizable as human. Lazy L brands were burned into her bleeding limbs, her bloody breasts, her belly; even her poor, ruined face.

He couldn't look anymore. His fist closed, crumpling the picture, and he dropped it to the floor. This was so far beyond anything he'd ever suspected of Loomis—so far beyond what he'd ever suspected any human being was capable of, not even when they were driven to madness by the butchery and terror of war—that he didn't have words for it, couldn't get a grip on his feelings.

But he knew, as he stood there in Loomis's torture chamber, that Loomis's plan for the women had only begun with getting them into that whorehouse of his. One by one, he realized, and by whatever means, Loomis would take them to this ranch, and to this room.

And they would never, ever come out.

"Slocum?"

Rance's voice sounded strange.

Slowly, Slocum turned to find him kneeling beside a chest of drawers. The bottom drawer, which contained what looked like several very large canning jars, was open.

"Oh, Christ," Rance groaned softly. He'd lifted out a jar, and he held it in his hands. "Oh, my sweet Jesus."

Slocum walked over and took the jar from him. He stared at it. The contents wafted and waved in their own restricted current as he turned it, trying to make out what was inside.

And then he could see, and he nearly dropped it.

Floating in the jar, suspended in a preservative liquid, was a crudely severed human head.

It was a woman's head, with long blond hair that must have been lovely when she was alive, before she came to such a horrible end. Her nose had been cruelly broken, bruises splotched her face, and there was a raw Lazy L brand burned into one cheek. Mercifully, her eyes were closed.

There was a paper label affixed to the lid of the jar. In a thin blue script, it read simply, "Julia Drummond, aged 23." this was followed by a date nearly ten years ago, and a single word, "Sweet."

The contents of his stomach rising up in his throat, Slocum slowly slid the jar on top of the bureau. He barely heard Rance over in the corner, puking up his layer cake. Probably his lunch from yesterday too.

This was where the odor was coming from, he suddenly realized. From the fluid Loomis used to preserve his trophies.

All he knew, as he blindly turned on his heel and started for the door, was that he was going to kill Loomis tonight. Monsters like this had no right to live, had no right to breathe the same air as decent folks.

"Gotcha, you sheep-murderin' bastard!"

Slocum went sprawling against a leather sofa, and saw a huge blade flash dangerously close before he could hiss, "It's me, MacGregor!"

The knife stopped an inch shy of Slocum's throat. "What're you doin' out here, mate?" Taggart MacGregor asked, seemingly not in the slightest upset that he'd nearly opened a new—and rather large—hole in his friend. He slid his knife away, then held a hand down, in the dark, to Slocum. "Easy up, chum."

"Thanks," Slocum said thickly, the contents of that locked back room still on his mind. He had a feeling they'd stay there for a good bit to come too. He picked up his hat and smacked it across one thigh. "And I might ask you the same."

"The bastard shot Miguel and killed 'bout half my woollies," MacGregor said, and for once there was no humor in his voice. "Thought I'd drop by and teach him a lesson. You teach him one already?"

"Not yet." Grimly, Slocum settled his hat back

on his head. "Waitin' for the sonofabitch. Me and Rance." He poked a thumb down the hall, and the sound of retching answered it.

MacGregor nodded his head. "Rance Peabody?" he asked, moving silently to the front windows. He peeked through the curtains. "Yeah, Mace told me about him 'fore those damn sheep killers came ridin' in. We got split up in the fight. Reckon him an' the others are out there somewhere, tryin' to rope what's left of my merinos in the dark."

Slocum nodded. "We saw your camp."

"Miguel still holdin' the fort, was he?"

Slocum hesitated.

Turning back toward him, MacGregor let the curtain drop. "Slocum?"

"Sorry, MacGregor," he said. "We put him up a cottonwood, temporary-like, so's the coyotes wouldn't get after him."

MacGregor didn't answer, but Rance, who had just come down the hall, said, "Somebody's out back."

23

Rance wiped at his mouth, then seemed to notice MacGregor standing in the shadows. "You sendin' out invitations, Slocum?"

"Rance, this is MacGregor," he said, swiftly turning on his heel. "MacGregor, this is Rance. All right? You girls can have the cotillion later on."

"I think that's prob'ly just Geraldo out there," MacGregor called, stopping Slocum in his tracks. "Ran into him on the way over. Told him to watch the back." He peeked out the front curtains again. "Nice t'meet you, Rance."

"Likewise," answered the gunfighter, although Slocum thought he still sounded shaky. "I don't reckon any of you fellers has anythin' resemblin' a plan?"

"Other than the one where Loomis is gonna be comin' into the yard any second with half-a-dozen hands and we're standin' around here pissin' down our legs?" Slocum asked dryly. "Not a one."

"Only half a dozen?" chirped MacGregor merrily. "No worries, fellas. We're on top of 'em."

A thin wail, originating in that horrible room

down the hall, suddenly cut the air. Slocum didn't know about MacGregor and Rance, but the sound nearly froze his bones.

MacGregor began, "Jesus! What the—"

"Our Chink friend," Rance said, cutting him off. "Musta woke up and saw where he was."

"Where was that?" asked MacGregor.

Curtly, Slocum said, "Well, go shut him up, Rance."

Over the screaming, which was quickly rising from a wail to a full-fledged shriek, Rance shook his head. "I ain't goin' back in there, Slocum."

"Goin' in *where*?" MacGregor asked.

"Aw, shit," Slocum grumbled beneath the din. He pushed past Rance and headed down the long hall, toward the only room from which light shone. And then, mindless of his throbbing arm, and keeping his eyes to the tiled floor—as if by not looking he could make it disappear, could force it to cease existing—he grabbed the bound Chinese cook by his feet and pulled him out into the hall, then slugged him into merciful silence.

He hadn't stood all the way up when Mac-Gregor hissed, "Riders!"

Quickly, Slocum reached in and grabbed the knob, shutting off the light from himself and the rest of the house. He went up the hall at double time, and when he came into the front room, he said, "Spread out and stay low."

There was a soft scuffle as Rance and Mac-

Gregor dove for cover—MacGregor behind the long leather couch, and Rance across the room, around the backside of an adobe pillar. Slocum drew his gun and took up a station about four feet down from the mouth of the hall.

In darkness, they waited.

Minutes passed, although they seemed like hours to Slocum. Outside, hooves scuffled closer and voices murmured, then gabbled, and he was aware of it, of all of it. But deep inside him, there was still a crawling sickness down in his belly, down in his bones. He had an inexplicable urge to just set fire to the ranch house, to all of the Lazy L, then toss himself in a horse trough to wash off the last traces of anything having to do with Loomis and his hobbies.

Hobbies!

He'd heard about men like Loomis. Well, not *exactly* men like him. He doubted there were more, or at least, he sincerely hoped there weren't. But he'd heard about a family in Nebraska—or maybe it was Wyoming—who killed folks that stopped by. Killed them and dressed them out and barbecued them, for God's sake, and buried the bones in the corn patch.

He'd read that by the time one of their intended victims escaped the roasting pit and brought the law down on them, the authorities found the remains of twenty-six men, women, and children in that cornfield.

He'd heard too about Skin Man Smith—hard to forget that name—who, when they found him up in Chicago, had collected the human hides—complete with hair—of twelve people.

Skin Man never went to trial. His neighbors in the tenement where he plied his "trade" had hauled him out into the street, then tarred, feathered, and lynched him.

Slocum didn't care to think what a man would want with human skins, let alone what would possess any man to take them.

Maybe there was something to those old-time beliefs after all. Maybe there were people who were possessed by the Devil.

Or were just evil incarnate.

Outside, boots crossed the porch, and then the front door swung in.

"Put him on the sofa," said a voice Slocum recognized as belonging to Loomis. "And for Christ's sake, don't let him bleed on my Persian rug!"

Loomis's figure turned to one of the two shadowy shapes following the two men bearing Barlow. That meant that there was at least one more, maybe two or three, somewhere outside. He tried to figure out which one was Sheriff Semple, while wishing he'd had the time—and the sense—to ask

Rance just exactly how many men Loomis had started out with.

"Light a lamp, for the love'a Christ!" Loomis said.

Light slowly rose in the room as the ranch hand lit the lamp and turned it up. Semple was nowhere to be seen. Was he outside, or had he been killed miles south, by the sheep?

Barlow groaned.

"Oh, shut your damn face!" Loomis barked. "It ain't my fault, you getting yourself gutshot."

Two of the other men exchanged quick glances that told Slocum they were having second thoughts about their current employment. Good.

And then Rance—showboating, as usual— stepped out into the edge of the lamplight, his gun drawn. Always one to jump right in for a theatrical entrance, was Rance.

"Sorry about that, Loomis," he said, and everyone turned toward him, Slocum included. "I was only aimin' to wing him, but he turned into it. You gonna be all right there, Barlow, you murderin' horse thief? Like to have you alive for the hangin'."

"Doctor," came the weak reply.

Slocum came forward next. Best to get in on the party. He said, "Reckon we'll do our best to get you one, Barlow, although I don't see as how you hardly deserve it. As for the rest of you boys," he added, looking Loomis straight in the eye, "why don't you come and take a peek down the hall, and then decide if you want to keep on workin' for your boss."

Loomis, his eyes narrowed, growled a warning, "Slocum . . ."

"Shut up, Loomis," he replied, and his voice was full of venom. "Men like you don't deserve to be called men. I doubt you're even high enough to be on a par with goat shit."

Rance waved his gun, channeling the hands toward the hall and past Slocum, who moved out into the parlor. He noticed that Rance hadn't disarmed them, or even tried to. Well, it'd be a moot point once they saw what their boss had been up to.

Loomis himself, however, was another matter.

"Toss those irons over easy," Slocum said. "One at a time."

"I'll get you for this," Loomis whispered, and his face was going fast to purple. "I'll track you down and see you hurt before I kill you, if it's the last thing I do."

"You gonna hurt me like you hurt those poor little gals?" Slocum asked through gritted teeth. "How many of 'em were there, Loomis? Fifteen? Twenty? More? How long have you been out doin' your evil in the world?"

Loomis spat at him, but said nothing.

Suddenly, there was a scuffling sound from the room down the hall, and the first ranch hand burst into the parlor. White-faced and terrified, holding his hands over his mouth, he raced past Slocum, threw open the front door, and proceeded to vomit over the porch rail. He was followed, in quick order, by the other three men.

They all had pretty much the same reaction.

Loomis paid scant attention. He seemed to be more incensed at Slocum's effrontery at exposing him than at the exposure itself.

"Doctor," moaned Barlow, oblivious to the upheaval going on around him.

"We'll get a doctor," said Slocum again, adding, "and the sheriff." Even a spineless dolt like Ward Semple would have to see that this was a real crime—a crime to beat all crimes. He'd have to do something about it.

One of the hands had wobbled up to lean against the front door frame. "How long, you evil sonofabitch?" he demanded of Loomis in a choked voice. "How long you been doin' this . . . this abomination? How long you been doin' it, right under our noses?"

He collapsed to his knees, sobbing.

MacGregor, who by this time had risen from behind his couch and was just standing there, looking curious, said, "Mind my askin' just what the devil is down the hall?"

Rance was just coming out, with Geraldo on his heels. Rance said, "You don't want to know, pardner. Trust me."

Geraldo nodded. He didn't look too well. "Just one glimpse, and I close my eyes. The Devil, he lives in this house." He made the sign of the cross, then turned to Slocum. "These are all of the men that rode in, Señor Slocum." He nodded toward the porch. "What do you wish I should do with them?"

Slocum was having second thoughts about Ward Semple. The sheriff was as weak as they came, and Loomis was a powerful man. He'd have friends in high places, friends who would never— *could* never—believe a word of what Slocum and the rest had seen here tonight, and who would take a few days to get here. A few days was more than enough time for Loomis to destroy the evidence.

It'd be his word against theirs. And Slocum was no fool. He knew that the word of a wealthy rancher like Loomis far outweighed anything they'd have to say.

After all, what were Geraldo and MacGregor but a couple of foreigners? What were he and Rance? Hired guns at their worst, roving paladins at their best. Hardly the equals of an upstanding citizen like Carl Loomis.

He knew what he had to do.

To the man hanging onto the door frame, he asked, "Where's he keep his money?"

"In the bank, I guess," said the hand dumbly.

"No, the cash on hand," Slocum said. "Where's he keep it?"

"I-in that empty flower jug," replied the hand, pointing across the room. "The old one, with them dragons on it."

"Don't touch that money, Slocum!" Loomis barked. "You're in enough trouble already!"

He was so far gone round the bend that he couldn't even see it behind him anymore. Slocum growled, "Shut up, you crazy bastard."

MacGregor, who was closest to the vase, handed it to Slocum, muttering, "You boys think you're gonna coddle me, do you?" and went down the hall. To have a look for himself, Slocum supposed, and he didn't try to stop him.

"Slocum!" warned Loomis.

"I said, shut up."

He dumped the contents of the vase out onto the tabletop. There was quite a bit of money, perhaps several hundred dollars. He started to pick through the coins. "What's he owe you to date?" he said to the cowhand.

The hand mumbled a figure, and Slocum counted the coins, then added thirty dollars. "That pays you to date, and gives you a month's severance pay to boot."

The coins fell with a clink into the man's outstretched—and shaking—hand.

"Now, grab a horse and get going as far and as fast as you can. And send in the next fella on your way out."

"Traitor!" spat Loomis, and his face was dark purple, his hands shaking with rage.

The hand just kept walking.

"Oh, Christ," came MacGregor's voice, muffled by distance and the hallway. Probably his hands too. "Sweet Jesus!"

Slocum just kept counting coins.

One by one, the men were paid, and one by one, Slocum heard them gallop off into the distance, a process interrupted only by MacGregor, who staggered back into the parlor, parchment-faced and muttering, "Dear Jesus, sweet Jesus," and looking for the whiskey.

"You men will pay for this," Loomis said, although anger had tied knots in his tongue and the words came out in a strange staccato.

"What next?" asked MacGregor, using his sleeve to mop the sweat from his brow despite the cool evening. He'd dropped into a chair opposite Loomis and Barlow, and his twice-emptied shot glass was in one hand, his knife in the other.

He was eyeing Loomis as a man might eye Satan himself, if Satan were made flesh and that man thought he had a good chance at gutting him.

"Now you and Geraldo haul Barlow outside," Slocum said. "The Chinese cook too. And go get your dog. She's hurt."

"What?" MacGregor was on his feet straightaway. "Which one? How bad is it?"

"One'a the black and white ones. And it ain't

so bad that I had to shoot her and leave her with Miguel,'' Slocum answered grimly.

"Compared to you, Loomis,'' MacGregor whispered with a sneer, "horseshit on the bottom of my shoe is just plain exalted. The Good Lord says we ain't to judge, that's his job. But I think he'll be forgivin' of me this time.'' He spat in Loomis's face, then turned away. "Where's my dog, Slocum?''

"Haven't you idiots done enough?'' Loomis fumed. He flicked the spittle from his cheek. "Get out! Get out of my house this instant!''

"She's out back of the smokehouse,'' Rance answered for him, ignoring Loomis entirely. "Leg's busted, I think.''

"Aw, Christ,'' MacGregor muttered sadly. "Poor girl. Poor little pelican.'' Without looking at him, he shoved Loomis aside none too gently and bent to grab Barlow's shoulders. When Geraldo took hold of his boots, they struggled out the door with him, Geraldo swearing softly in Spanish the whole time.

"All right, Loomis,'' Slocum said to the rancher, who was silently fuming. Rance came forward too. "I think it's about time we shut you up.''

24

Loomis had plenty of reasons to be afraid, but he had no sense whatsoever. In the center of that room he'd built, the chamber of tortures in which he'd slowly taken so many anguished human lives, he stood facing them: weaponless, friendless, without a single ally.

Yet his expression was smug, so smug that for a moment Slocum wanted to strap him up in his own gear, to see him flogged and welted and bleeding.

But he didn't. He'd be damned if he'd sink to Loomis's level, which was pretty damned low indeed.

But he said to Rance, "Hook him up in a set of those cuffs."

Rance complied. He stepped back, his brow furrowing momentarily, and then it cleared. "Gonna whip him, Slocum?" he asked almost gleefully.

"No," Slocum said, and forced himself to go to the bureau that contained those jars. "Just don't want him to jackrabbit out of here. I'm goin' to take a little inventory, if I can stomach it."

"Oh, screw you and the horse you rode in on,

Slocum," Loomis spat suddenly, flailing his arms in the manacles. "You're all cowards, the lot of you! I thought you were big stuff! Why don't you act like it?"

Slocum turned toward him. "And do what?"

"Take this thing out in the yard," Loomis roared. "Gun it out, you sonofabitch! Either that, or shoot me here and now!"

Loomis was enraged, but Slocum saw that it was a different rage from before. That had been mindless fury at having his grisly trophies seen by outsiders, at having intruders in his home, and his money pilfered. He hadn't been furious at having been found out, so much as at having to share his toys.

Sick? Loomis was sick, all right. He had a malady that had long ago taken what was left of him mind.

But now Loomis's fury was turning to frenzy—frenzy at the thought of being subjected to even a small dose of what he had subjected others to in this, his own made-to-order corner of Hell.

"Gag him," Slocum said.

"You can't!" Loomis cried in sudden panic.

"My pleasure," replied Rance, and pulled a leather gag down from the wall.

Loomis's cries were stifled as Rance fitted the gag over his mouth, and Slocum turned once again to the bureau. Slowly, he began emptying the drawer of jars, and then another drawer, and another.

Rance was trying not to look. He said, "Slocum? What you got in mind?"

The drawers were emptied, and the jars that they had contained—and that contained, in turn, floating clouds of once-burnished blond and brunette and red hair, wafting slowly about ruined faces that would see no more, would never laugh or cry or kiss a baby—lined the floor and bureau top.

One jar in particular stopped him cold. He recognized the name written on the lid, written in a casual hand.

Slocum, his eyes clouded with tears he would not shed, said, "Get Geraldo and MacGregor in here."

After Rance gratefully took his leave, Slocum wiped at his eyes with a rough thumb, and then he turned to face the man who had done all this, and whose eyes now bulged in terror. His attitude had changed, all right. Good.

"I don't know how long this has been goin' on," Slocum began, "but I reckon it's been a long time, maybe since you were out of diapers. And I don't know that this is all of 'em, all of the women you hurt and tortured and terrified and killed."

Against the gag, Loomis said something undecipherable. It didn't matter. Nothing he could have said would've made any difference.

"What I do know," he continued grimly, "is

that this is gonna end tonight. No more. Never again. You know, you could've kept this up for a long time if you hadn't got so greedy. We found out about the gold.''

Above the gag, Loomis's eyes bugged out.

"It's a good strike," Slocum said evenly. "Maybe even better than the stuff they were mining before. But you were a rich man, Loomis. If you'd left their sheep the hell alone and backed off the gold, I never would have found you out for the greasy snake you are. You could have had it all—the gold, the women, everything. You probably could have had the sheep too—killed or run off or sold off—if you'd just taken your time. But you couldn't wait, could you? Personally, I'm right glad you're such a greedy bastard.''

He felt his hands balling into fists, his nails digging into his palms, but he wasn't done yet. "You're plain evil, Loomis, Satan himself come to earth. What you did to Jane, up Chicago way, that was just a taste, wasn't it? Just a taste of what you gave poor Ann-Elizabeth, and what you were gonna give Charity. Your own niece! And then maybe Jane and Maddie too. Jesus Christ Almighty, I swear I wish I could kill you fifty times over, and that each time it'd hurt worse the time before!''

"Slocum?" It was Rance. He, along with Geraldo and MacGregor, were waiting in the hall.

Shaking with rage, Slocum growled, "Get in here," through clenched teeth.

Slowly, eyes downcast, they shuffled into the room.

"Hats off," Slocum said, and willed himself back under control.

Each man removed his hat and stood waiting.

"Boys," Slocum said, "we ain't got twelve men for a jury. We only got four, plus the four that peeked in here earlier and puked their guts out. That's eight, and enough for a jury in some parts. I figure those boys that took off each registered a 'guilty' vote. Seem that way to you?"

"*Sí,*" said Geraldo, still staring at his boots.

"Right by me," said MacGregor, his face pale and stony.

Rance just nodded.

"I reckon then, Loomis, that we oughta count off the names of the victims, such as we know 'em, before we finish pronouncin' the sentence. Maybe it'll let these poor little gals rest easier up in heaven. And maybe it'll shove you deeper down into the fires of hell."

He picked up the first jar and its macabre contents, and read the name. "Dolores Sanchez, aged thirty-six," he said. Then the next one. "Susan Butler, aged fifteen."

MacGregor took a step toward Loomis, but Rance pulled him back.

Slocum continued solemnly reading the labels,

trying to keep his mind on what he was doing instead of what he was handling, trying to focus on the women these had been, rather than what Loomis's diseased games had turned them into. Darcy Pepper, aged twenty-two. Angelica Romano, aged twenty-one. Maria Elena Domingo, aged nineteen.

The dark hair of Running Fawn, encased in glass and fluid, swirled beneath his fingers. The light hair of Sarah Carmichael still had a pink ribbon snared in its sodden tangles.

At one point, he stopped, thinking he couldn't go on. But then Rance's hand brushed his shoulder, and he heard MacGregor mutter, "Chin up, mate."

And he went on. Twenty-two jars, twenty-two lives nipped away. The last was also the most recent. Ann-Elizabeth Fleming, aged twenty-four, killed less than a year ago. Maddie's friend.

He didn't know how he would tell her.

Gently, he set the jar down beside the others.

Aside from Loomis's tortured breathing, there was silence in the room for a moment.

MacGregor was the first to speak. "Rest in peace, ladies," he said softly.

"Yeah," said Rance gruffly, his voice thick. "Sleep in the arms'a Jesus."

Geraldo crossed himself and muttered a prayer under his breath.

"How say you all?" Slocum asked.

"Guilty," said MacGregor.

"Guilty," said Rance.

"*Sí*, guilty," said Geraldo.

"Guilty," Slocum said. "It's unanimous."

MacGregor sighed, then looked over at Slocum. "What now? You want I should skin him out?" His fingers twitched, probably itching to unsheathe his blade.

Behind the gag, Loomis protested violently. To a man, they ignored him.

"No," said Slocum, as much as he would had liked to turn MacGregor loose on Loomis. "Start splashing kerosene."

Leaving Loomis to shriek against his gag and twist in his bonds, they started through the house, emptying lamps against floors and paintings, splashing them against drapes, over beds and chairs and tables.

At last, they returned to Loomis's torture room, ready to douse it too.

"Wait," said Slocum, holding up a hand. "Leave the lamps and kerosene out in the hall for a minute."

The four men gathered at the door, three of them looking to Slocum for direction.

Slocum gave it.

"Form a squad," he said, closing the door against the kerosene fumes that filled his nostrils. They'd slosh this room too, after they'd done what was needed.

Without a word, the four men drew their guns and spaced out, in a line.

"Ready."

The guns came up. Loomis found his tongue again, but all that came to their ears was his hysterical, but mercifully muffled, screech.

"Aim."

Four guns settled on their target, four hammers cocked as one.

"Fire!"

Dawn was inching over the horizon as the four men walked solemnly down the front steps and out into the crisp predawn air. MacGregor had loaded his bitch into the buckboard already—a buckboard with the word O'HARA neatly burned into the side—and she thumped her tail against the seat at the sight of him.

The Chinese cook was just coming round—again—and Geraldo helped him to his feet and untied him. Shakily, he looked round at the men. "What . . . ? What . . . ?" he stuttered.

Slocum reached into his pocket and pulled out the last of Loomis's jar money. He handed it over and curled the cook's fingers around it.

"Your boss ain't gonna have no more need of a cook," he said flatly. "This here's your severance pay. This, and a horse. Pick one out of the corral, and then go as far away from here as you can."

The little man bowed and started for the corral, then stopped. "In locked room," he began. "What I see. He do that? Mr. Loomis do that?"

Slocum nodded.

The cook spat. "I take two horses," he said, and disappeared in the morning gloom.

"Barlow's dead," MacGregor stated flatly. Slocum looked toward the wagon, where MacGregor was just dropping Barlow's wrist. He jumped off the wagon, and began hauling the body off the tailgate. No one objected.

"Wonder what's become'a them boys and the Mex that went out to check the sheep," Rance said, then caught himself. To Geraldo, he said, "No offense intended, amigo."

Geraldo nodded curtly. "None taken, Señor. I am wondering the same thing myself."

Rance said, "I'm wonderin' about the sheriff too. Didn't Geraldo sling Barlow here up behind the tin star over to your place, Slocum?"

They all turned as the sound of approaching horses, which turned out to be the cook— mounted, and leading not one, but three spare horses. "Change my mind," he announced. "I take three extra. One for every year I work here. Anybody objecting to this?"

No one did.

"Good," he said. "The one I ride, I take in trade for my possessions inside. I not go back in house. Very bad, very bad. No one is objecting to this also?''

Again, the men remained silent.

''Okay, okay,'' said the cook, who was obviously still rattled. Slocum understood. They all were. ''How he do these things?'' the cook went asked. ''How he do and not make noise? There is no noise!''

''The walls,'' Slocum answered, staring at the horizon. ''Those walls were adobe, three feet thick.''

''Outside walls, yes,'' said the cook. ''Inside walls, no.''

Slocum sighed. ''Inside walls, no. Except for that room. Three feet thick, and no windows. He planned it, the sonofabitch. He built that house thinking that he'd . . .''

He let it trail off. He was thinking about Maddie and Jane and Charity, thinking about how they might well have ended like the hapless Ann-Elizabeth: kidnapped, tortured, and killed, her epitaph nothing but a question mark.

Until now.

Behind him, he heard the scuffle of hooves as the Chinaman rode away, leading his string. Hell, he could have taken every horse in the corral for all Slocum cared.

''Hey, Slocum?''

It was Rance.

"Yeah," Slocum said, and began rolling himself a quirlie.

When it was licked and ready, he stuck it in his mouth, flicked a lucifer into life, and lit it, then tossed the still-burning match onto the kerosene-soaked porch.

As they watched, flames raced into the house on a damp, flammable highway.

Adobe don't burn worth a damn, he was thinking as they watched the flames begin to ripple at the windows, devour the curtains, race up the paintings, crack the leather furniture.

No, adobe don't burn worth a damn, he thought as he turned away, *but it sure as hell makes a good oven.*

25

They rode into Maddie's place mid-morning, toting the body of Miguel and an embarrassed Sheriff Semple, who had a broken leg—suffered not a half mile from Maddie's front porch, before all the hoorah got under way. They'd come across him—full of questions, which they didn't answer—on their way in.

They'd come upon Pablo and Mike and Mace about an hour after leaving the Lazy L. The trio had mercifully escaped any injury, and were busy looking for the scattered sheep with the aid of MacGregor's two remaining healthy dogs. Around seventy-five head had been chased out of the brush so far, roughly half the flock.

MacGregor had wanted to stay and oversee the operation, but Mace surprised Slocum by saying—with no small degree of pride—that he believed he had this sheep herding thing figured out. And besides, MacGregor looked like he'd been dragged for two miles—why didn't he get some sleep and some decent chow?

They answered Mace's questions about the smoke billowing on the horizon the same way they had later answered Sheriff Semple's: To a man, they said they didn't know a dad-blamed thing about it.

Slocum's arm, still sore from the slug Barlow had put into it, became sorer still from all the shrugging he was having to do.

But it was better. They all agreed. Nobody would believe Loomis's crimes without proof, and nobody should have to see that, see the terrible sins of which a mortal man was capable.

Slocum knew he'd never put Maddie through it anyway.

And so they'd made a pact, as they were riding away from the flames. They'd never tell anyone what they'd seen. Never.

"My buckboard?" Maddie said after she'd kissed Slocum silly, then scolded him for making her worry so long and so hard. "Where'd you find my buckboard? I haven't seen it since that un-grateful Ann-Elizabeth took off in it!"

And then she saw the solemn look on Slocum's face, and she said, "Come inside."

He slept until it was nearly dark, and the room had grown dusty gray. Odd to wake up to the sounds of supper being made, and to the sun going the wrong way in the sky. But he sat up, letting his age-battered body parts set their own pace for coming awake, and finally swung his legs down to the floor. His arm was sore, but it didn't look as if it had been bleeding. One more scar to add to the many.

He'd live.

He dressed, and made his way to the front room. Rance was there, red-haired and fastidious as ever, and lounging beside the hearth with his feet stuck out toward the middle of the room. He greeted Slocum with a lopsided grin. "Howdy, *compadre*! Finally decided to join the living?"

Maddie turned from the big iron oven and came toward him, wiping her hands on her apron. "Hello, darlin'," she said, and gave him a peck on the cheek. "Don't listen to that old Rance. He just stumbled out about a half hour ago."

He gave her a hug and a pat on the bottom, nodded a hello to Jane, and then tipped his head in Rance's direction. "Want to stretch my bones," he said. "Care to take a stroll, Rance?"

Together, they walked out into the dusk. Geraldo was just coming up from the abode brickworks, dusting his hands on his shirt, and he joined them.

He nodded. "Señores," he said.

"Howdy," Slocum said. "Where's MacGregor?"

"Back with his damn sheep," Rance replied around the cigar he was lighting. "Took Charity with him. Well," he added with a grin, "maybe she was the one doin' the taking. He seemed mighty happy to be took too."

"Sí," Geraldo echoed. "Mace, he comes to the house at noontime for food and brings much mutton with him, for the ladies. Then Señor Mac-Gregor goes out to the flock and takes with him Charity, also a meal fit for a king. That Pablo! He is eating good!"

Then he remembered himself, and added, "They need Señor MacGregor to help skin out and bury the dead ones. The sheep, I mean. Mace, he says they find more alive since this morning. Ninety altogether, I think—but it sounds to me like that is all they are going to find."

Slocum nodded. "Well, that's more'n half, anyway." He dug into his pocket for his fixings, and when Rance offered a cigar, he turned it down.

"Ask me again after supper," he said, rolling a quirlie. "The women. They ask any questions?"

"Asked about the buckboard, I heard," Rance said.

Geraldo added, "Señor MacGregor, he tells them that we find it deep down in a canyon. He tells them we find Señorita Ann-Elizabeth's bones too. He says we bury them and bring back the wagon."

Slocum nodded. He'd told the others about Ann-Elizabeth on the ride back, so MacGregor had been prepared for the questions. It was as good a lie as any.

"They ask about the fire over to Loomis's place?" He found he could hardly say the man's name without choking on the sudden rush of fury that rose up his throat.

Rance said, "Same as last night. We don't know squat, and we're stickin' to it. I hear the sheriff left for town in the buckboard 'bout an hour before I got up. Mace drove him in. Oh, the ladies set his leg this mornin', by the way. Got quite the tender hands with things like that, those gals."

He grinned. "Seems that ol' Ward Semple was near as puzzled as us civilians about that conflagration up to Loomis's."

"Nobody went racin' out there to put it out?" Slocum asked.

Geraldo wagged his head. "We are the closest to the Lazy L, and it is three miles from us. Some men from town, they went, but it was too late. Frank Bloom—he is from the tobacco shop in town? He rides through here on his way home. He tells us there is nothing left but the smoking shell by the time they got there. No hands, nothing. Just a few horses in the corral, and no buildings touched except the house."

He shrugged, and then wiggled his eyebrows. "It is a mystery, is it not?"

Puffing on his cigar, Rance nodded. "Yup."

They all turned at the distant clatter of an approaching buckboard. It was Mace, clipping along the road from town, a haze of dust following him in the approaching darkness.

Everything's back to normal, Slocum thought.

Ain't it strange how everything goes right back to normal? He ground out his smoke, then turned on his heel, starting back toward the house, and the others followed.

"Slocum?" Rance asked.

"Yeah?"

"Seem odd to you? I mean, hell's bells! Didn't you sort of expect the sky to turn some ungodly strange color? Maybe the voice'a God hisself to come booming outta the clouds?" Rance shook his head. "Just seems odd, everythin' being so ordinary after . . . after that hellhole last night."

Slocum didn't speak right away, but Geraldo did. "Señor Rance," he said, "I think we are very tiny in the eyes of our Lord. I think we are very tiny, but what we did was very right. I think we could do no other, and I also think He would commend us. It is not for me to say, but perhaps He already has. And life?" He hunched his shoulders, then let them slump. "She goes on."

"Yes, she does, Geraldo," Slocum said as they came to the porch steps, to the sounds of animated female chatter and the smells of roasting mutton and fresh-baked biscuits and green beans with bacon. "She goes on."

And so do I, he thought.

Time to be moving on down the trail.

That night, after Maddie and Slocum had made long, slow love, she turned to him. Framed by the moonlight filtering through the window, she said, "Slocum? It's a bunch of horseshit, isn't it? What you men told us, I mean."

He put his arm around her, and she pillowed her head on his chest.

"Don't know what you mean, Maddie darlin'."

"All that stuff and nonsense about finding the buckboard in a ravine or a canyon or whatever it was MacGregor said. My stars, that buckboard no more went over the edge of a canyon than I did! And about finding Ann-Elizabeth's bones. About knowing nothing about the fire at Loomis's place. You're not telling me the truth."

He hugged her closer, and kissed the top of her head.

"Never could keep a damn thing from you, Maddie," he whispered. "Even when it's for your own good."

"Tell me, Slocum."

He sighed. "Darlin', you don't want to know, not really."

"Yes, Slocum," she said. "Yes, I do. Tell me."

He thought for a moment. He loved her, he supposed, as much as it was possible for him to love. Loving was in his nature, but sticking around wasn't. He need to wander like most men needed food.

He knew that, as did Maddie. He'd be leaving in the morning, but he wouldn't leave her with the same memory he had, the memory that he knew would steal his sleep for countless nights to come.

"I killed Loomis," he said, starting with a truth, or a partial truth. "I found your buckboard in his barn. I was waitin' for him in his parlor when he got home, and when I confronted him, he admitted . . . he admitted that he'd waylaid Ann-Elizabeth and killed her."

Maddie sat up, holding the bed linen about her like a shield. "But why? Why on earth would he kill her? We weren't feuding, not back then. We were still digging gold and I hadn't even thought about bringing in sheep and Loomis hadn't yet come up with that lunatic water rights scheme."

Slocum's hand went to her arm. He was glad it was dark, glad she couldn't really see his eyes and the lie in them.

He said, "It was an accident, Maddie, but he covered it up and buried her somewhere on his ranch. I don't know where. And after he admitted it, he drew on me."

"You were faster," she said. Not a question, a statement.

"I was," he said, then added, "Loomis's bullet went wild, hit a lamp. The whole place was in flames before I hit the front door."

But Maddie wouldn't let it die. "And Loomis's hands?" she said. "They say the place was deserted. Where were his man when you two were shooting at each other? Where'd they go to?"

"I don't know, Maddie," Slocum said. He

rubbed her back, silently coaxing her to lie next to him again. "He rode in alone, and I rode out alone with a fire at my back. That's all I know, honey."

She lifted her head until her lips were at his ear, and then she whispered one word.

"Liar."

Her hand ran down his chest, then over his belly, tracing old scars and ridges of muscle, to gently grasp his cock. The other hand was at his cheek. She kissed him, tenderly at first, and then with a rising fervor, until he was stiff in her hand.

"Thank you, Slocum," she murmured against his lips, between kisses. "Whatever you did—and I have my doubts about that cock-and-bull tale you just told—thank you."

Despite himself, Slocum felt a chuckle rise up his throat. It was the first inkling of levity that he'd had since he'd walked into that terrible room at Loomis's the night before, and it felt unaccountably good.

Laughing softly, suddenly feeling happy out of all proportion, he wrapped his arms around her and flipped her onto her back.

"Slocum!" she said, feigning shocked surprise. "Whatever are you doing?"

"Cock-and-bull story, eh?" he said with a grin. "Well, madam, let me introduce you to the rooster end of that little phrase."

To the accompaniment of Maddie's bubble of

laughter, he plunged into her, and made love to her for the last time.

He didn't wake her to say good-bye. He hadn't told her he was going, but she knew. She'd known last night, even though she hadn't said anything.

There'd be no good-byes between the two of them, no sloppy fare-thee-wells. He knew he'd be back someday, and she knew it too—at least, he hoped she did—but when that someday might come was anybody's guess.

He found Rance in the kitchen, dressed and ready to ride, and filling a napkin with leftover biscuits. "Morning, Slocum," he whispered as he grabbed two more. "You thinkin' what I'm thinkin'?"

"What? That we want to retire to someplace with palm fronds?"

Rance made a face at him. "Be serious."

Slocum snorted. "South sound good to you?"

"Fine an' dandy," came the reply. "Them gals down Tombstone way have got to be missin' me somethin' fierce by this time. Why, I wouldn't be surprised if the management over to the Birdcage just up and gave me a free pass upstairs!"

"Then I suppose we better get you down to Tombstone," said Slocum with a smile. "I feel sorry for those poor doves, just pinin' for your company."

He opened the front door. "C'mon, get your

thieved biscuits wrapped up. I want to be on the trail by sunup.''

"Hey, Slocum?''

He turned back.

''Hear they got some damn good haberdashers down there,'' Rance said. ''Long as we're gonna be in Tombstone anyway, why don't you let me buy you a new goddamn hat?''

A smile lifted one corner of his mouth. ''C'mon, Rance.''

As they rode out at an easy jog, the dawn rising rosy-pink on the horizon at their sides, he turned in the saddle one last time to look down upon Maddie's ranch. And he thought, as he gazed out into the distance, that he saw a figure standing in Maddie's bedroom window: a lone figure, waving a hand slowly.

And even though he was fairly certain it was just a trick of the light, or an overactive imagination, or even wishful thinking, he lifted a hand and waved back, just once.